$ BLOODY MONEY 2 $

The Game Ain't Fair!

A Novel By:

Leondrei Prince

STREET KNOWLEDGE
PUBLISHING

Website: www.streetknowledgepublishing.com

$ Bloody Money 2 $.

Published by: Street Knowledge Publishing
Written by: Leondrei Prince
Edited by: Joseph L. Jones
Cover design by: Kenny Briscoe/ A6
Media/www.a6media.com
Photos by: Shorty Wright

For information contact:
Street Knowledge Publishing
P.O. Box 345
Wilmington, DE 19801
E-mail: jj@streetknowledgepublishing.com
Website: www.streetknowledgepublishing.com

ISBN 10: 0-9822515-9-9
ISBN 13: 978-0-9822515-9-1

Table of Contents

Acknowledgements

First and foremost, Allah is Akbar! I give all my praises and success to him. Without him, none of this would be possible for me. I want to thank all my fans for supporting me from day one. "Bloody Money 2" is for y'all. It's my way of saying thanks. I hope y'all enjoy it. Again, this book is for the "Red Brick City". Long live "Riverside, Bucket, Two-six" and to my angel, my daughter, Ms. Khalia Thomas... Love ya!

I want to give shout outs to "Turf" today. All my peoples from "2-4" and 23rd Streets. Much love to y'all for keeping it "'Hood" 365 days a year. To my li'l cousin, Boomer, hey, baby! My boy, Kontel

A.K.A Gates or Peacock, much, much love to you, Akee! To my boy, Qwazoe. Cousin Al (Big Guy). To my crew, cousin Sly D, Ed Lover. The boah, Crack, Shizz, Ellis, Stevie, Wonderful, the boy, Bar, Big Mar, Old School, Li'l Var, cousin Sha'mar, and everybody else I missed up. Turf, much love. Cousin Shawn (S-Dot) McNeil, Lil Ant, and Burn-Burn. To my baby Earl (E.S.) Snead, hey Cousin!

To my New Castle crew, how can I forget y'all? Cousin Daytime, Ghetto, Richie, K.B., Kenyatta, Brian Turner, Kenny (Bin Laden) Land, Anthony Terry, Jamal Pinkston, Malike Miller, Slash, J.R. White, James Sullivan. My partner, friend, and li'l brother, Mr. Joseph (Joe-Joe) Jones. You got the best writer on the East Coast. The numbers will prove it this year. My li'l cousin, Fresh Mally A.K.A Big Jamal. Cousin Tony Washam, love you, boy! Tylynn, hey cousin! To my boy, Rashann (B.L), Wallace Evans, Vernon (Sleepy) Johnson, Ira (Lil Daddy) Shay, and Big Shock, hey cousin! To my Chester Boys: Cholly AK and Fitz, much love. The boah, Mookie Too, and Harper.

To my Hilltop family, y'all know who y'all are. I shouted y'all out in the first two books. To the C.B.W., wha's good? My boy, Philly Tarron, and Shannon Brown, wha's up nephews? To my cousin, Damon (Lil Coston) and Jose, thanks. Thanks for loving me when I just needed a hug or a shoulder to cry on. To the West Side. To the Cage 1. The entire Delaware gets love form me all the time. I rep us in every city I go to. I put is on the map! I did it because I'm not a hater. If half of y'all was more like me, you wouldn't have to hate either because you'll have your own, feel-me?

To Riverside, the projects. Hey family! Much, much love to the boah, Butter Rico, we miss and love you, baby boy. The 'hood just ain't da same for gangstas. To my baby, Doo Doo A.K.A.The Beast, say what they want nephew, but keep it to their selves, or else! (Ha-ha!) To my baby brother, Booder-Bontae, hey cousin, much love to you. Keep doing your thing. To my baby, Boop A.K.A Beedie Beep, to Fatty A.K.A. Goat. My baby ABE A.K.A Pain, I love you, nigga! To my niece, Lil Neeka and her posse, Monique and Key Lo-Lo, wha's good? To the boah, Rocko, the boah, B-Neil Speedoc, Lil Boop. Jazz-o, hey li'l sista! To my cousin, Snook A.K.A Spunk, who loves you, nigga? My baby, Monk A.K.A Double R, China Man, Shebo, Dadda Boy. To cousin, Jay

A.K.A Jihad, Poop-Lips A.K.A. Lipers. To my li'l cousin, Bobby Dimes, love you, boah! To my baby, Prada A.K.A D-Akavelli A.K.A Knock Out Artist, much love to you, you crazy mu'fucka! To my baby, Murder. Li'l Dullah, Pete Rock, Boog A.K.A Young Grams. To all the li'l soldiers coming up, stay strong, and stay focused. To my baby, Mark (Saint) Stewart. If I missed anyone I apologize, then again, I probably already got y'all before. To my boy, Ziare (Ziggy).

To my Crest Roses, some very beautiful females I was locked up with in a program. Keep y'all heads up and stay strong! Ms. Angela Sicilliano, the world will know you soon! Ms. Ocean Christopher, Ms. Katrina Thomas, Ms. Barbra A.K.A Pocahontas, Ms Chastity Zimath, Ms. Lanora Brown, Ms. Mayo, my counselor, Ms. Gholston and Ms. Inez, and to my baby, Ms, Latisha Minor, much, much, much love to you baby! Damn we make beautiful music together, huh?

Last but not least, this shout out if is for a true friend of mine, a person special to me, someone who no matter how bad they know it will hurt me still says the shit anyway. A person who, whenever I go to jail, accepts all my collect calls and never complains. A person who loved me since the moment we meant as kids, teen-agers. A person I love to this day, despite whatever. A person who expects the best out of me because she sees my potential, and I see it too now. This one is for my future wife and fiancée, Ms. Wheatina Goodman. I love you baby!—Sike! I'm just bullshitin'. Those gossip loving mu'fuckas would have loved to run with that one! Pick y'all's mouths up, it's only a joke (Ha-ha!). But seriously though, Wheat, I do love you and I appreciate you being my friend. Thanks sincerely, your Dog A.K.A Lee-Mudd. Hey cousin Tash and Aunt Nelly, love y'all too. Hey cousin Doggie-Dog!

Now to my fellow writers: much love to my two Ace-Boon-Coons in this writing world, Mr. Al-Sidiq-Banks, and Mr. Treasure Blue. I know I ain't gotta say it, do I? To Mark Anthony, Eric Grey, Shannon Holmes. To my girl, Ebony

Storman, my girl Tanya Nuez. To my sista, Ms. Kashamba Williams, your advice is working. I'm cutting people off slowly but surely. Much love and much success in all that you do. To all the distributors who carry my books, thanks for getting me known to the world. All the street vendors and Black bookstores who support Leondrei Prince, I thank y'all too. Much love…

Peace! I'm out!

Dedication

This book is Dedicated to all my fallen friends and loved ones whose lives were cut short in some way or another by the results of chasing that "Bloody Money". May you all Rest in Peace.

"The Sistas"

Ms. Deborah (My Mother) Prince
Ms. Nate' Owens-Hollis
Miss Lakayla Booker
Ms. Neka Owens

"The Brothers"

Mr. Trans Owens
Mr. Howard (H-Town) Brown
Mr. Michael (Def-Jam) Brown
Mr. Kenneth (Love) Davis
Mr. Rick (Big Rick) Glasgow
Mr. Kevin (Kev) Conners
Mr. Troy (X)
Mr. Michael (Majic) Bland
Mr. Michael (Mike-Mike) White
Mr. Johnny (J.C.) Jackson
Mr. Pierre Carter
Mr. Kevin (Back Catcher) Smoke
Mr. Larry (Tight-Feet) Davis
Mr. Waali (Gator) Bey

Mr. Damon (George) Emory
Mr. Shawn (Dr. O) Owens
Mr. Purnell (Lovie-Love) Green
Mr. Gregory Graves
Mr. Barry (C.A.B) Wilson

Love and miss you all!

Leondrei Prince

Chapter One

The phone was ringing as she sat on her knees, hunched over the toilet throwing up her lunch. "Damn it!" she said to herself between a gag and a dry heave. "What's wrong with me?" This was the second time today she found herself praying over the porcelain god, vomiting her guts up, and the episodes were becoming more and more displeasing as the reality of her intuition was manifesting itself right before her eyes. But she still had hope that it wasn't true.

She walked out of the bathroom directly across the hall from the closet and grabbed what she had bought at the Wal-Mart nearly a week ago, the first time she missed her menstrual cycle. Reading the directions on the box carefully, she re-entered the bathroom to clear her conscience and to answer the question that went unanswered for the past two months or so; was she pregnant? She took the plastic test kit out of the box and grabbed the little strip that contained a mark for her to urinate on, and squatted to pee.

"Damn!" she said as urine ran over her hands and the strip. *At least the majority got on the strip and not my hand,* she thought as she wiped herself and stood to place the strip back into the test kit.

The moment she placed the strip back into the test kit, she began pacing the floor. Instantly, time seemed to stop, and the five minute wait became more of and eternity as she waited for the results to come clear. When she pulled the strip from the test kit, her heart dropped down into her stomach as the blue positive sign stuck out to her as clear as day. Jennifer Vault, A.K.A. Lucy, was pregnant.

"Oh my God!" she panicked. "What am I going to do?" she asked herself, as other questions began to flood her mind: *How am I going to explain this to my family? What will my mother think? Then again, to hell what they think. I'm tired of pleasing them. That's why I resigned from my old job, because I'm tired of pleasing them. It's not about them anymore, it's about this child I'm carrying and how good of a mother I can be to it. How is he or she going to be able to deal with the fact that they're interracial? How will he or she be able to deal with the ridicule of being mixed by its peers? What will I tell my family about the child's father? Oh, that he's a black guy who's five years my junior? No, that will never work; then again, it'll have to work, because it's the truth!*

Lucy was suddenly exhausted, mentally drained and couldn't wait to go lie down somewhere; anywhere. All the thinking and worrying she was doing about her newfound discovery wasn't going to change anything. She was still pregnant. *I have to go lay down somewhere,* she thought as she scratched her scalp. *The couch, the love seat, the bed, the floor... anywhere!*

Lucy stood in front of the sink, looking down at the plus sign on the strip, mesmerized. She turned on the cold water and placed her hands underneath the spout and splashed the water she held cupped in her hands onto her sweat-soaked face, and felt alive again. But then the tears started. It was the first time since she drove through the tollbooth entering Maryland that she cried again, because she had placed him in her past. He was gone, it was over, and that chapter in her book called "Life" was supposed to be done, but it wasn't. Pretty E wasn't a part of her past, he was here right now.

The phone rang again. By the time Lucy made it down stairs to the phone, it had stopped ringing again. She pressed the button on the caller I.D. and noticed that the last two calls were made from the same number with a 302 area code. Delaware, she remembered. *It's him! No, I'm not calling the number back. I'll tell him about the baby later. No, I'll never tell him about the baby. Yeah, 'cause that way it will be easier for me. I won't have to deal with him or see him and risk having my feelings caught up on him again,* she thought, but the phone rang again. "Damn, it's him!" She looked down at the phone, and out of instinct she answered it with trembling hands. "Hello!" she answered with a crackling voice.

"Hello, may I speak to Lucy?" the voice on the other end asked.

"This is she. May I ask who I'm speaking with?"

"This is Rasul, Lucy. How are you doing?"

"Rasul, oh my God! Like, is it really you?"

"Yeah, it's me."

"Where's Eric?" she asked, sensing something wrong.

"That's what I'm calling you for. Him and Dog got in a little trouble."

"What kind of trouble?" she asked, trying not to sound too frightened.

"Well, a couple days ago the police stopped them, and well, you know…"

"Know what, Rasul? Come on, tell me what's wrong."

"They got knocked off."

"Knocked off? With what?" she asked, knowing the slang term for getting arrested from her undercover days.

"With two keys and some guns."

"What?"

"Yeah, and the lawyer couldn't even get them a bail."

"The lawyer couldn't get them a bail?" she asked.

"Nope!"

"Well, fire him then! I'll take over the case now. I'm their lawyer," she said. The protective side of her took over as she thought about her lover sitting in some cage. "How long have they been in jail?"

"Three days."

"Three days! Oh no, that's definitely too long. By the way, how did you know how to reach me?"

"I found your letter, the one you slid under the club's door."

"You didn't read it, did you, Rasul?"

"No, I didn't read it... *Ms. Vault!*" he said, letting her know that he had read the letter.

"I'm going to kill you, Rasul!" she said playfully, and then assured him she was on her way. "Rasul, I'll be there tonight around nine o'clock. I would be there earlier, but I have to wait until this rush hour traffic dies down."

"Did you say nine?"

"Yes, nine o'clock. What I need from you now is your contact number."

"Don't you got caller I.D.?"

"Yeah."

"Well, that's my number; it's my cell phone."

"Okay then, I'll see you at nine."

"No, you'll see me tomorrow morning."

"Why?"

"Because, I'm in Florida."

"Okay, well, I'll see you then."

"Okay."

"Good-bye," she said, and hung up the phone.

Lucy flopped down on the couch next to the end table where the phone sat, and tried to digest the news that Rasul had dispensed to her. When it rains it pours!

She thought about everything that was happening in her life. From the pregnancy to the love of her life, down to her new career as an attorney, Lucy's life was in total disarray. She didn't know what move to make next, but she did know one thing. She knew she had to get her baby out of jail. Just a few months ago, she wouldn't have been caught dead even entertaining the thought of saving what society called a "criminal," but Pretty E had changed all of that for her. She had officially changed over to the other side of the game. The side that she was taught as a child to avoid, to shun away from, wasn't what her parents said it was. They had taught her that the people living any other way than they were living was wrong.

However, as she grew older and came to find herself and Pretty E, she knew she had been misled. The good old American pie way wasn't always a reality. There was a side where you had to stretch five nickels into forty cents, a dollar into two, and one meal that could feed a family twice and have leftovers. That was the reality, and that's what Pretty E brought to her life. She understood now and gained a whole new aspect on life, one she never had before. She had a balance to weigh out options, choices, and decisions about a matter, giving each side an equal opportunity, and this matter was no different. But it was all one sided, all in favor of Pretty E.

She had to defend him and Dog, because she knew there was no lawyer in the world capable of doing the job she could do, because it was personal. This was someone dear to her, and a way to clear her conscience of what ate at her mind every single day; the suicide of Hakeem (Hit Man) Stewart. She knew it was her fault he was dead, because she put her pressure on him to go against his will, and he couldn't live with himself anymore. For that, she felt as though she would always be in debt to Rasul, Dog, and especially Pretty E.

Lucy got up from off the couch and headed to the kitchen to grab another slice of the pizza she was eating for lunch. Snatching a paper towel from the roll on the wall, she paced the pizza slice on it, and set the microwave to twenty five seconds. Her stomach was growling and her mouth began to water as the aroma escaped the microwave. *That must be the baby,* she thought, and a huge smile covered her face as her hands found her belly.

■■■■■■

"...Locked up, they won't let me out,
And I had a long day in court.
Shit stressed me out!
Can't get me a bail, and can't get me out,
Now I'm headed to the County.
Gotta do a bid here,

I'm used to living luxurious,
I don't want to live here..."

Akon, Featuring Styles P
Locked-Up

Dog and Pretty E were handcuffed together as they were led from the courthouse and piled into the court van. Eleven other inmates were already stuffed in the small Ford van and ready to get back to their cells, far away from the courthouse that was trying to put another obstacle in their already mixed up lives. When they boarded the van, the ever so real lyrics from Styles P were coming out of the factory system that the guards had tuned to Power 99 FM, and they struck a cord inside the both of them. The more the song played on, the more it applied to Dog and Pretty E, but it didn't just apply to them. It applied to each and every man and woman caught up in America's justice system, whether it was just or unjust, and the song was just that real.

"Yo, did y'all come out right?" an old head from around the way asked them as the van left the garage and headed down 4th Street.

"Yeah, we straight, ol' head. They just denied our bail, that's all," Dog said.

"For what? Y'all ain't killed nobody."

"Come on, ol' school. You know how them mu'fuckas do," Dog answered.

"I heard dat. Y'all's lawyer couldn't do nuffin'?"

"Nah man, the whole police force was up in there. Them mu'fuckas was talking about shit that didn't have nuffin' to do with this case, feel me? We got knocked for some other shit, not for no bodies and shit, you know? The guns they found ain't have no bodies on them, so I don't know why they came at us like that. Either way though, we're going home, you know?" Dog finished.

"Yeah, ol' school, when your money is right, you don't even have to worry about cases and shit. All you gotta do is wait 'em out," Pretty E added.

"Yeah, and stick to the rules of the game. Keep ya mouth shut and make 'em prove their case," Dog added as the van pulled into the garage off of 13th Street into Gander Hill's Booking and Receiving.

One by one, they were escorted off of the court van and placed into a barred sliding doorway leading into the jail, while the guards went through a regular door to unarm themselves of their weapons so that they could enter the prison to un-cuff the inmates.

Just the smell of Booking and Receiving alone was enough to make Dog and Pretty E's stomachs turn with disgust. They couldn't believe that they were in jail. Their run had finally come to an end, and for the first time since Ferris School for Boys, they were captive again.

"Wha's wrong?" the guard asked the both of them as he un-cuffed them.

They didn't respond. They were too busy trying to brainstorm a way out of their situation, and at the same time, adjust to their environment, as they were led to a holding tank.

"Damn man! Can you at least leave the door open?" Pretty E asked as the guard shut the door in his face.

"You should have stayed home," the guard replied sarcastically.

"Fuck you, pussy! You ain't hard to touch! Nigga, you know who I am?" Pretty E snapped.

"Yeah, I know who you are. According to this paper here, you're Inmate 202254," he responded, and walked off.

"Fuck you, house nigga!" he yelled at the guard's back.

"Man, fuck dat nigga! Don't get yourself all upset over that shit, man. We only here momentarily. The next time we go to court we'll bailed out, cousin. Just relax," Dog said.

"Man, we might not go to court for another two or three months, man. I ain't for this shit!" he said. "And this shit either!" he finished as he observed the holding tank.

Cellblock Number 141 was the largest holding tank in the Booking and Receiving area of the prison. Two long steel benches ran down each side of the walls, and a stainless steel sink and toilet sat in the corner right next to the short bench. The other wall was empty, besides the three Plexiglas windows that were built into it, and every inch of the cell was occupied. The stench in the cell was nearly unbearable, as bums lay stretched out with their shoes off, and smelling like cheap wine and sweaty feet. Dope-sick junkies were bent over, clutching their stomachs out of pain from withdrawing from heroine, and periodically racing each other to the toilet to free there systems' of the poison by vomiting or releasing their bowels. It was unexplainable to a person who had never seen a dope fiend going through withdrawals, but it was definitely something you didn't want to see.

"Man, I gotta get the fuckup outta here!" Pretty E said, frowning his face up at a junkie as he vomited into the toilet.

"I feel you," Dog added, as a guard came in and opened up the door.

"Benson! Harrison! Williams! Lollie! Wright! Davis! Allen! Cook! And Riley! Come on, you're going back to your pods, tiers, or whatever you want to call 'em, but your getting up out of here," the guard yelled into Cellblock 141, and the inmates called began filing out.

Dog and Pretty E were glad that their names were called, because they wanted to get the hell up out of the room.

"Who are you?" the guard asked as they filed out of the cell.

"Benson," Pretty E answered as he fell into the single file line.

"And you?"

"Lollie," Dog responded, and fell in behind Pretty E.

The guard led the inmates down the hall in a single file line towards general population.

The only good thing about the whole situation was that they had pull with the guards who worked in the prison. Half of them they had sold drugs to before they became who they were, and the other half could be bribed with a couple dollars. One of them, a guard in Booking, had already made sure they were on the same tier and in the same cell. It was like that in any city or state you were in inside the penal system. The guards were as slimy and crooked as any of the inmates they were hired to oversee. There was nothing in jail you couldn't get, from pussy to oral sex to drugs and cell phones or weapons. It didn't matter. Everything was just a bribe away from switching from their hands to the inmates' hands. It was just that simple.

The crazy thing about it all though, was that even with all the luxuries you were able to obtain in jail, nothing was sweet, nothing at all. You were still in jail, in the can, in the slammer, in the bing, in the box, in the joint, or whatever else you wanted to call it, so again, it wasn't sweet. In jail, you are locked up, captive, away form your loved ones, and missing out on time of an already short life.

Jail was miserable, and Dog and Pretty E were reminded of that the moment they stepped on their tier and saw what they had seen for the past three days that they were there. They saw muthafuckas doing the same thing they did everyday—absolutely nothing!

"Wha's up, cousin!" Kevin asked them the moment they came on the tier. "How y'all make out?"

"We did all right. They really ain't got nuffin' on us, but so many people came to court, they denied us bail," Dog replied."

"For what?"

"For nothing," Pretty E said before asking Dog to go get the guard to crack open their cell door.

"Why you trying to go in the cell?" Dog asked.

"'Cause I want to holler at you for a minute."

"All right, but we might as well stay out here 'cause it's almost count time."

"It is?"

"Yeah. Plus, there ain't no telling if we going to come back out or not, knowing these mu'fuckas. You know they don't like coming to work."

"Oh shit, that's right! We don't come out if it's one guard, huh?"

"Yeah, that's why I ain't trying to go in the cell right now, 'cause ain't no telling if we coming back out. I hate being caged in."

"I feel you, cousin."

"Well, let's go play some Spades or some 'em then," Dog said, and they walked over to the table where a Spades game was going on.

"We got next," Pretty E said as they walked up to the table.

"Well, you know what you gotta do, cousin," one of the dudes said while holding out a piece of paper and pen towards him. "Keep score."

"I heard dat," Pretty E said with a smile as he grabbed the piece of paper and pen.

■■■■■■

The Orlando sun was out and shining brightly as usual, bringing the weather up into the mid-90's. Rasul refused to let the phone call Tameeka received from Tammy a few days ago about Dog and Pretty E's arrest put a damper on his get-away. This was his time, the time he needed to reflect on his life and the direction it was headed in. He was way too young to be going through what he was going through at such an early age. The stress, worry, and paranoia that came with the game could drive a normal person insane, but it was the life he chose to hustle, and there was no turning back. He had already, in his young twenty-five years, been shot at, jailed for eight years, and lost his best friend to the life he chose, *but who said da game was fair?* he asked himself when he hung up the phone with Lucy.

Rasul stood in the kitchen in front of the sink and stared out the bay window at the beach. What he saw was the beautiful blue water and a skyline that looked like a prism, displaying the colors of the rainbow. Actually, as the waves splashed and the water rose onto the shore, it kind of reminded him of the movie "Point Break" with Patrick Swazey and Keanu Reeves. The only difference was that this wasn't a movie; this was real life—his life.

He thought back on the days when he was caged in the cell with Frankie, learning a whole new game, and was glad he did because the game he and his boys were living in and playing with was a dead end. They would have never reached the level they were on now, or seen the kind of money they saw now. They were all millionaires a few times over, and all this happened in just a little over two years.

Damn! Rasul thought to himself, amazed that he accomplished nearly every goal he set out to achieve while in jail in record time. Twenty-four months, three million and some change, multiple businesses, stocks and bonds, plus a beautiful wife, and a child on the way was virtually impossible for a "ghetto child" unless you hit the Power Ball or some shit. But not for Rasul. Simply, hard work, dedication, patience, good money management, and a strong connect put him and his boys in the pros. But, they were greedy, and their greed almost cost them everything they worked for in just a matter of seconds.

"I'm done!" he told himself. "This game ain't worth me going back to the box and losing everything I got," he reasoned as he looked out on the beach at his wife and stepson bathing in the sun.

Rasul walked outside through the back sliding door, stepped onto the deck, and took a deep breath of the oceanfront air. The past three days had been absolutely refreshing to his body and soul. It gave him a chance to really relax for the first time since he'd been home from McKean Federal Prison.

"Baby, can you bring me my Prada shades off of the counter for me?" Tameeka yelled from the beach when she noticed her husband coming down.

"What counter?" he asked

"The kitchen counter."

Rasul walked down the deck of the house onto the beach, carrying his wife's sunglasses and two bottled waters.

"Thank you, baby," Tameeka said as she grabbed a bottle of water and her sunglasses. "And what did I tell you about wearing those ugly things all the time?" she finished, talking about the prison shower shoes he always wore.

"What, these?" he asked, looking down at his feet.

"Yeah, those!"

"I told you that these are my reminders. They help keep me focused. Helps me remember the times when I was caged like some animal. See baby, it's real easy to forget where you come from once you get out of jail because you free again.

Why do you think so many people keep going back and forth to jail?"

"I don't know. It only took me that one time to go for them credit cards, and I said, never again!"

"It's easy for y'all to say never again, because y'all are women. Y'all don't have to do nuffin' because y'all have a pussy."

"So, what you sayin'?" she asked, agitated.

"I'm sayin' a nigga will break his neck for a woman, and she doesn't even have to be all that pretty. All she has to do is play her cards right."

"Whatever!"

"For real. Look at it. The government gives y'all Section 8, subsidized project houses, all dat shit. But the niggas, we don't get shit! Feel me? Mu'fuckas don't give us nuffin', so we gotta go hard or just be ass out. So, what I'm trying to say is that we don't keep running back and forth to jail 'cause we want to, we just lose focus, start chasing the easy way when shit gets rough, and by doing that, we jam ourselves up repeatedly, that's all. So baby, that's why I wear these muthafuckas all the time, 'cause I ain't going back!"

"It shouldn't take no damn shower shoes to make you not want to go back to jail. You should just not go back. Damn, how hard is that?"

"See, that's what I'm talking about. I just sat here and broke everything down to your ass, and you still gotta be sarcastic or some 'em. Look, never mind that shit. Let's just move on."

"Damn, why you gotta get mad? I only said it because it doesn't make no sense that a pair of damn shower shoes gotta keep you focused. That shit is weak!"

"Maybe it's weak for you, but for me, it kept me out for over two years, so I ain't going to stop wearing them now."

"Okay, okay, damn! Why is you still going on and on and on about it? Just leave it alone."

"Because you always trying to get the last word in, that's why."

"Well, wha's going to happen to Dog and Pretty E?" Tameeka asked, cutting him off and getting the last word in anyway.

"I don't know. We'll see when Lucy comes back to Delaware."

"Lucy? That's the Fed bitch, ain't it?"

"Yeah, that's her, but she ain't no Fed no more. She's a lawyer."

"A lawyer! How you know that?"

"Because before she left, she left a letter."

"Why would she leave a letter to you, and where would she leave a letter for you to get?"

"The letter wasn't for me, it was for Pretty E," he answered, and then caught himself.

"Pretty E! Why would she leave a letter for him?"

"Why are you asking so many questions? Damn!" he said, knowing she was onto something.

"Mmm-hmm, a dirty muthafucka, huh! He probably done fucked da bitch. I can't wait to tell Tammy," she said, her attitude switching up just like that.

"You better not do no bullshit like that. That man ain't fuck that woman."

"Well, why did she leave a letter?"

"Because she feels guilty about Hit-Man's death, that's why. She feels like it's her fault that Hit-Man killed himself, so since she became a lawyer, she feels as though she needs to represent us in any illegal shit we get into."

"That's bullshit! 'Cause if it was going down like dat, y'all would have never hired that other lawyer. So, wha's up with that?"

"'Cause I just got the letter."

"Yeah right! Screw my head back on when you finish."

"Girl, you crazy!"

"You think I am, don't you?" she said, and rolled her eyes. "That's a shame too, 'cause you're probably just like him."

"Come on baby, don't do that to me. You know damn well that my heart don't pump no love, lust, or desire for nobody but you," he said, and she melted. It was the little things like that he did all the time that made her feel special. To her, Rasul was as sweet as a bag of cotton candy brought freshly from the carnival.

"Baby, I love you," she said

"I love you too," he answered, and gave her a peck on the lips.

Chapter Two

Lucy packed up the last of her belongings in her Coach suitcase, grabbed her briefcase at the door, and headed out, off to Delaware for her first big case.

She had passed her test for the Bar at law school with flying colors, the same way she did at the federal offices, earning her the right to practice in Maryland, Delaware, Pennsylvania, and New Hampshire. So it was nothing to state to the courts that she would be representing Eric and Michael.

The only thing that bothered her now was how long it was going to take for her to get them a new bail hearing. That was always the problem in the court system of Delaware; getting a court date. The jails were so over crowded that the judges were backed up for months. Sometimes it took two to three months to get before the judge on a driving case, so something of this stature could take up to a year before the trial could even began. That's what Lucy was afraid of. *I'll go straight to the commissioner's office,* she thought as she placed the last of her belongings in the trunk.

Lucy weaved the Maximum in and out of traffic smoothly, almost a choreograph, as the car floated up I-95 North.

She reached up in her sun visor and grabbed her Marlboro Lights, then held the red hot metal rings to the tip of her cigarette and took a long pull. "Oh my God!" she panicked. "What am I doing?" she said as she rolled down her window and tossed the cigarette. "I'm sorry, baby," she said, and rubbed her potbelly before tossing the whole pack and focusing on the obstacles ahead of her.

She had more than butterflies, she had more like humming birds as she thought about a hard fought trial. From what Rasul had told her, Eric and Michael had been caught red-handed with two thousand grams of cocaine— the equivalent of two kilos—and some automatic weapons. She knew from cases like "Williams vs. California," "Mitchell vs. Texas," and even our own "Joseph Jones vs. Delaware," that probable cause had to be proven in cases like this.

Also, why were they searched anyway? Did they run a stop sign or traffic light? Did, after the stop, the police see a weapon in plain view, or see or smell any drugs? Just what exactly did they do to warrant a search of the vehicle they were in? These were just some of the questions that were racing through her head.

Then, there came her biggest obstacle, the Delaware judicial system, the one that made up new laws every day. The law that introduced T.I.S. (Truth in Sentence) to the nation requires inmates to do 85 percent of their time, the ones whose jails were busting at the seams with probation and parole violators, because of a poor system designed to keep grown men in jail and off the streets. The laws whose self defense law was exonerated, and the one whose laws allowed innocent people to be convicted at trial by hearsay, and the list goes on and on. That was Lucy's biggest fear. She feared that she would lose a hard fought trial to an unjust system that strives for a high conviction rate.

Lucy parked her car on 5th Street, directly across from the new courthouse, and walked across the street. Her mission was to wait for the Court Commissioner to come in, if he wasn't there already. Lucy knew that bail was a must, except in capital murder or federal cases, but they hadn't stepped in yet, so she had to move fast.

The courthouse was nearly empty at nine o'clock in the evening, except for the night guard and two secretaries in the municipal court office.

Lucy stepped swiftly across the freshly waxed floors, her heels tapping oddly, sending an echo through the huge building as if there was someone following her. A sense of fear overcame her, as it would have anyone who was into scary movies like she was. The quiet of the building, its stillness and dark hallways kind of reminded her of the long hallway in the movie the "Shining" where the two little girls were riding their tricycles.

Lucy spun on her heels and was relieved. "Ssshhhwww!" she sighed with her hand on her heart at the sight of the janitor coming up behind her. *Thank God! It's only the maintenance man!* She laughed at her silly thought, and entered the municipal court office.

Inside the office, one of the two secretaries was filing and copying paperwork, while the other one sat behind a desk arranging subpoenas to be mailed out in the morning. Lucy, looking sleek in her Liz Claiborne skirt and blazer, placed her suitcase on the front desktop and asked the lady licking envelopes for some help. She flashed her Attorney at Law business card and proof of identification by showing her driver's license, then asked for the court docket sheet of today's arraignment in which bail was denied for Eric Benson and Michael Lollie.

"I'm sorry, Ms. Vault, but can you please repeat that for me?" the secretary asked, handing Lucy her license back.

"I need the files on today's court procedures in which bail was denied for Eric Benson and Michael Lollie."

"Hold up a sec. Let me go pull that up for you."

When the secretary handed Lucy the files from today's court hearing, she saw where the judge had went along with the State's recommendations by labeling them "Kingpins." The docket sheet, as she read along, explained more in detail on how the police officers knew them from confidential informants and from run-ins they themselves had with them.

The police officer who did the most damage though was Detective Cohen. He held the judge, prosecutor, and everyone else in the courtroom captivated by his statements, as he went along in detail of what he thought about the two accused. He told the court of a robbery/homicide in the Hilltop section of the city. He spoke of a disappearance in which a Shelly Kamota and her boyfriend, Bobby (Bo-Bo) Bonds, had been missing for over two years. He spoke of the murders that took place in the Colony North Apartments, in which their now deceased friend was charged with, but nothing he spoke about had anything to do with the drugs or guns found in the vehicle.

"That bastard!" she thought aloud, seeing how a judge could deny bail. "He shouldn't have allowed that testimony in the bail hearing," she said to herself as she remembered the time she first met the detective at the hospital.

Detective Cohen was now the head of homicide at the Wilmington Police Department, a job he was promoted to after the murder of his partner, Detective Armstrong. She knew by the way he acted when she stepped in as lead federal agent on what he thought would be his case, that he had it out for Dog, Rasul, Pretty E, and Hit-Man. *He probably even went as far as to do some illegal shit to get them,* she thought, and remembered just how unjust the Delaware penal system was. Everyone was corrupt, from the judges, to the lawyers, down to the accused. The lawyers even worked deals with the prosecutors on occasion, giving their own clients up to lengthy plea agreements. It was just like that, and as a result, many men, women, and families were suffering behind the friendship of an attorney and prosecutor's friendly little agreement.

The more she read on, the more their case had the characteristics of a railroad written all over it. "Rasul called me in the nick of time," she told herself, as the thought of Pretty E being railroaded was unimaginable.

Lucy had enough of reading the blatant setup and was ready for war. The adrenaline rush she felt right now was the same one she felt when she netted the largest drug bust in east coast history. She felt victorious, and wouldn't settle for anything else but a victory. To lose wasn't even in her vocabulary.

"Excuse me!" she said, calling the secretary back to the front desk when she was finished with the docket sheet. "When is the Court Commissioner due back in?"

"He should be back in any minute now."

"Fine. I'll just have a seat then."

■■■■■■

The Court Commissioner came into the office at nine-forty five p.m., but Lucy wasn't called to go back into his chamber until a little after ten o'clock. She stepped through the door, and the commissioner stood to his feet and offered her a seat, which she respectfully took.

"Hello, Commissioner. My name is Ms. Jennifer Vault, the new attorney for Mr. Eric Benson and Mr. Michael Lollie," she said with an extended hand before taking her seat.

"Hello, Ms Vault. I'm Commissioner Spacey," he introduced himself and took her hand.

Lucy pulled out the court docket sheet and began reading off what she had highlighted earlier. The contents of what she read were so interesting to him that his usual laid back persona was awakened.

"Hmm," he mumbled under his breath as the attorney read on. He couldn't believe what he was hearing. It was totally unjust to have had all those people testify at a bail hearing, and the defense attorney not once set out to object all the allegations.

Lucy knew her stuff, and by the way the commissioner sat up in his seat, she knew she captured his attention. The more Lucy stated her facts and beliefs to Commissioner Spacey, the more he respected her position. He also knew right from wrong, and he knew the law. There was no way in the world that the judge should have allowed all that testimony by those officers, and there was no way that their lawyer shouldn't have tried to defend them from it.

"Do you know what I'm going to do, Ms. Vault?" he asked, not waiting for a response. "I'm setting a new bail hearing for tomorrow at 9:00 A.M."

"Thank you, Commissioner, thank you for being fair!" she said, pleased with his decision.

"You're welcome, Ms. Vault, but it's not necessary for you to thank me. I chose to follow my heart on this decision, that's why I'm in this position. I'm in this position because I'm a fair person, and I know that everyone is entitled to a fair trial. It's an Amendment right," he replied and stood to wish her well.

"Thanks again, Commissioner," she said with a huge smile before turning to leave the chamber.

Lucy was all smiles as she high-stepped out of the courthouse on 5th and King Streets. The first part of her uphill battle was won because she got them a new bail hearing. Now all she had to do was get them a bail that was reasonable. "I guess I'll go share the good news with my clients," she said to herself as she swung the corner of 4th Street in the direction of the prison.

■■■■■■

Wilmington, Delaware is a small little city, barely visible on a map, and the center of the Tri-State area. If you were traveling north to south, or south to north, there was no way you could bypass the tiny state, because I-95 runs right through it.

Lucy took in the sights as she drove, and nothing seemed to have changed. The only thing that looked different to her was the ever growing bank of M.B.N.A. and the building up of Delaware's River Front. She smiled because the memories she had here were still fresh in her mind: She smiled because this was where she found herself—the self that suppressed its own happiness, its own beliefs for that of others. She smiled because this was the city that showed that self how to live again. She smiled because she was free, happy, and fresh out of the shell she's been in for so long. She smiled because she finally found that inner peace that been missing from her life ever since she gave up her power to her family and stopped making decisions on her own.

Lucy turned onto East 13th Street and saw the ever so familiar Gander Hill Prison sitting off to the left of the street, and a lump formed in her throat. The only thing she could think about was how bad the guards were treating the inmates behind the maze of barbed wire fences, brick, and steel. *I hope they're treating my Eric right in there,* she thought as she parked her car in a near-empty lot. No sooner than she exited the car and her foot touched down on the pavement, she heard the inmates banging on their windows, screaming out obscenities at the top of their voices. She ignored them.

Lucy walked into the prison lobby, and the first thing she noticed was the name change painted on the wall, which read, "Howard R. Young Correctional Facility". *Ha! What a joke!* she thought to herself. The real name should be, "The

Howard R. Young Correctional Facility," she determined. She remembered the stories she had heard about the prison and the people in it, from the one about the guards smoking crack, to the illegal fucking between guards and inmates, all the way down to the records department in which a couple dollars could change your release date. The whole institution was crooked.

"May I help you?" the guard at the desk in the lobby asked.

"Yes, I would like to see my clients. I'm an attorney," Lucy replied, reaching for her I.D.

"I'm sorry, Ms. Vault," the guard said, grabbing her

I.D. "But I'm afraid that's going to be impossible right now.

The facility is in code red status.

"What's that?"

"The prison is locked down until tomorrow."

"But I'm from out of town. I just came all the way from Oxin Hills, Maryland. I only need a few minutes."

"Ma'am, what part didn't you understand? I said the prison is on a lock down status. I wouldn't have cared if you drove from Florida. That wouldn't have changed the fact that we're locked down right now. You're going to have to come back tomorrow," the guard said sarcastically.

"No, I'm not coming back tomorrow. I'm going to see my clients now… or do I have to call the commissioner and have him personally order my visit?"

"Like I said, Ms., the facility is locked down, and frankly, I don't care who you call!" he replied, and spun around on her leaving her standing at the desk.

Lucy couldn't believe the nerve of the guard who so rudely left her standing at the front desk to go finish a game of Solitaire he had saved on a computer. His antics felt more like a slap in the face than just some blatant disrespect, and she was going to set out to prove that some facility lock down wasn't enough to keep her form seeing her clients. She grabbed her cell phone from her handbag and began dialing the number for municipal court, and heard the familiar voice when it answered.

"Hello, municipal court. Jackie speaking." "Hi, Jackie. This is Ms. Vault, the attorney who just left the commissioner's office.

"Oh, Hi, Ms. Vault! Is there anything I can do for you?"

"Yes, in fact there is. Can you please transfer me to the commissioner's extension, please?"

"Sure," she said, and after a short pause followed by a couple of rings, the commissioner answered the phone.

"Hello, Commissioner. This is Ms. Vault, the one who just left your office."

"Hello, Ms. Vault," he answered.

"Commissioner, I'm calling because I've run into yet another fork in the road. It seems that the people in charge here at the Gander Hill Prison won't authorize a visit for me to see my clients. You know my situation, Commissioner, and I want to know if there is any way you can assist me in this matter," she asked politely.

"Are you there at the prison now?" he asked.

"Yes."

"Okay, hold tight for a minute. I have to make a few calls," he assured her before disconnecting himself from the phone line.

"Okay," she said, before the line went dead.

Lucy looked at the guard sitting behind the computer and waited until they made eye contact with one another before she reacted to his rudeness. She smirked at him, rolled her eyes and spun hard on her heels causing her hair to swing before going to take a seat in the lobby.

Damn, dat shit looks good! she thought, digging for some change in her purse as she stared into the vending machine. This had been happening often lately, where she would catch cravings for food and junk food that she hadn't eaten in years, and the moment she heard the coins tumble down into the belly of the machine, she knew it had to be the baby. She reached down into the mouth of the machine and grabbed her Raisinets after she punched the code B-9 on the machine's panel. And no sooner than she tore the edge of the wrapper to pop some into her mouth, the guard was coming from behind the computer to get her.

"Ms. Vault!" he called out to her. "Right this way, please."

"Thank you!" she said with a smile.

■■■■■

"Code red! Code red! This facility is now in a code red status!" the voice sounded over the prison P.A. system, and then the guard inside the bubble on the tier clicked the doors open. The sound that the doors made when they clicked the pen had the same effect on the inmates that a snap of the fingers had for a physiatrist's patient under hypnosis. It brought them back to the here and now. The sound always reminded them that they were indeed in jail, and even the little bit of recreation time that they were allowed to have wasn't even guaranteed to them.

"Come on now, y'all. I know y'all heard me click the doors. Y'all ain't stupid, y'all know what it means. Y'all better lock in them cells or I'ma start writing y'all up!" the guard threatened.

"Fuck you, bitch!" someone yelled as they scrambled to their cells.

"Y'all really going to be calling me a bitch tomorrow when I don't let y'all out at all, so keep talking shit!" she snapped.

"Sike, Ms. Williams! We just playin'," the inmates said, grabbing cards, chess pieces, and checker boards to lock in their cells with them. They did this because this was the last time for tonight that they'd be out of their cells until tomorrow, so cards, checkers, and chess was a must for them to have in their rooms, because a six by nine jail cell could sure become boring real fast.

"Dat's what 'cha mouth say!"

"For real, Ms. Williams!"

"Alright, alright, just lock in. I don't want anybody on my floors except my tier men," she spoke, and the floor emptied.

"Benson and Lollie, y'all stay out too. I want y'all to help my tier men," she finished, and they looked at each other and smiled. They smiled because the guard working their tier was Kareema Williams, a young girl from north side that their young boah, Slash lieutenant, Shay-Ball was fucking. She was supposed to make the drop-off to them today, so it must have been a go. The only thing they had to do now was stay under the radar when and if she actually passed off, and that was the crazy part. You would think that since you were in jail you would be able to do some illegal shit and get away with it, but that wasn't true. You had to watch out for the other inmates the same way you had to watch out for the guards, because they were just like the police. They would tell on you for nothing at all, but they'd mainly do it for brownie points. Brownie points would get them good jobs in the prison, plus build their jackets up to look good at classification hearings to get them home faster or sent to a half-way house.

"Cousin, you think she got dat shit on her?" Dog asked as he stood at the 190-degree waterspout, pouring water into their bowls of soup.

"I don't know," Pretty E said, draining water from a can of tuna fish. "She probably do."

"Pretty E!" she called over the loud speaker, then motioned her hand for him to come to the bubble.

"Alright," he acknowledged her by holding up one finger. "Yo, Dog, I'ma go see what she wants, so finish up this for me," he said, sliding him the tuna fish.

"Alright," he said, and gathered everything up and headed to the cell.

Pretty E walked over to the bubble and knelt down into the mail slot to talk. He kept his back turned towards all the cell doors on the tier just in case she had to pass off, then he asked, "Wha's up?"

"Here, boy, take this shit," she said, and pushed the paper bag through the mail slot into his hands.

"Thanks, baby girl! That's good looking too, hear? Oh, and tell my boy I said wha's up! Alright?"

"Alright, I'll tell 'im. But you need to holla at him, because I'm about to cut his ass off, you feel me? I could've stayed with that other nigga for all dis shit. You just don't know how much shit Shay-Ball be putting me through."

"I heard dat. Just hold on, though. I'ma holla at dat nigga, okay? Tell 'em to get his shit right."

"Hmm, if he don't know by now, he won't ever know, 'cause I'll be gone," she said, then continued. "Y'all be careful, okay?"

"You know it."

"Alright then, I'll see y'all tomorrow."

"Alright," he said, then turned to leave. "Oh yeah," he said spinning back around. "What chu eating for lunch tomorrow?"

"I don't know. Why? You want me to bring you some 'em?"

"You know I do. Bring me a sub or some 'em."

"I got you."

"Don't forget!" he replied, and headed to the cell.

Pretty E peeped through his cell door window at Dog, who was sitting behind the metal desk with the stool in front of it, mixing the soup, rice, cheese, mayonnaise, tuna fish, and whatever else you decide to mix in it—from honey to hot sauce—before entering the cell. He waited, because in reality, it was his turn to make the jailhouse delicacy called "Tuna Buna", and he didn't feel like making it.

"Wha's up, cousin? Did she bring it?" Dog asked when Pretty E walked in.

"Yeah, she brought it."

"Was it all in there?"

"I don't know, I ain't check yet," Pretty E answered, pulling the bag out of his pants.

"Well, check it then, nigga! I'm trying to call my wife."

"Yeah, it's all here," Pretty E said, pulling out a cell phone, Dutchies, a lighter, and an ounce of haze.

"Let me see that phone, nigga," Dog said as he reached for the Nextel. "Is it any extra batteries in there?"

"Yeah, it's some in here," Pretty E answered, looking into the bag.

"Good," Dog said, and dialed his house number.

Kim answered the phone on the first ring like she was sitting there waiting for it to ring. "Hello!" she spoke into the receiver, anticipating his voice.

"Hey, baby! Hi! Wha's up?" he answered.

"Oh my God, baby! I miss you!" Kim said.

"I miss you too!"

"Why haven't you called me?"

"Because these muthafuckas is playing with the phone system shit."

"Well, how did you call me now?"

"From a cell phone. Didn't you see the caller I.D.?"

"I didn't give it a chance to register a number before I answered."

"Yeah, well, that's how I called."

"How'd you get a cell phone?"

"How you think, baby?" He didn't wait for an answer. "One of the guards bought this shit in."

"Oh!"

"What's my kids doing?"

"Nothing. Getting on my nerves with all these damn questions. I guess they must be starting to feel that something is wrong, because they are asking about you and why you haven't been home."

"They are?"

"Mmm-hmm, especially Li'l Mama," she said, talking about the baby.

"How's Li'l Mike?"

"He's okay, but I swear to you, Michael, he acts just like a grown man. He's the one who is really acting different. It's like he knows that you're in some kind of trouble, and he feels the need to step up, like he's the man of the house or some 'um, you know? He's been coming out to the car when I pull up like, 'Mom, you want me to help you do this or do that?' Or he be like, 'Mom, do you want me to wash my li'l brother up in the tub for you?' He does all of that, baby. That's my baby! That's 'Mommies Li'l Man'!" she finished before asking, "What happened in court?"

"They denied our bail—" and before he could finish he heard her crying.

"What are they going to do now? What am I going to do without you? Oh my God, what are we going to do without you? Baby, me and the kids need you!" she rambled on between sobs.

"Calm down, baby, calm down. I'm fine. They really don't even have a case against us."

"That's bullshit, baby, 'cause if they ain't have a case, they would have gave y'all a bail. Oh my God, what are they going to do?" she asked frantically, thinking the worst. She knew how hard Delaware was when it came to drug charges, because they gave her cousin, Carron, eight years just on an indictment, so imagine what they were going to do to them for two kilos and some guns, she thought and began to sob heavily.

"Baby, I said we're going to be alright."

"I'm getting you a different lawyer."

"Baby, relax. I'll let you know what moves to make, alright?" he said as her sobs began to make him feel unsure. "Look, let me go, alright? The guard is coming. I'll call you the next time I get a chance, okay? 'Cause I definitely ain't supposed to have this cell phone. Look, I love you, hear?"

"I love you too."

"Kiss the kids for me, and tell 'em I love 'em."

"Okay."

"Oh, and make a visit."

"I already did. It's for Sunday, and I sent you some money. Okay?"

"Okay, baby, let me go."

"I love you!" she said, blowing kisses through the phone.

"I love you too!" he said, and did the same.

"See ya!" she said, and hung up the phone.

"I love you too, nigga!" Pretty E teased and blew a kiss.

"Fuck you, nigga! Roll a Dutchie!" Dog said.

"I already did, nigga. What? You want to light it?"

"Yeah, put some fire on that muthafucka!"

■■■■■■

The guard in the lobby called for another guard to come and escort Lucy upstairs to see her clients. She had been to the prison before, but never went beyond the walls of the receiving room, and as she walked through the halls she wondered about all the people who she had put in jail. She wondered whether, if in fact, any of them were like Pretty E; people who had been oppressed by the invisible hands of the U.S. government, and who really had no other means than to do what they had to do. The U.S. government had a way of gluing anyone's back to the wall who was either uneducated, an ex-felon who was trying to make a change, or people of the two or three minority races. The good old American way life was only in Hollywood. Only in Hollywood could a person lose everything they got in one day, and gain it all back and more in only two hours or less.

When they reached the second floor of the prison, the guard made turn after turn through the prison maze of clicking and sliding doors, until they reached the front door of 2-F pod. Lucy watched as the guard kicked the bottom of the pod's outer door hard and repeatedly before it clicked open like the other doors they just came through.

"See this door here?" He pointed at another door that sat in between pod's 2-F and 2-G.

"Yes, this door right here," she replied.

"Yeah, stand right there in front of it while I go inside and get it open. As soon as you here it click like this one just did, go inside and your clients will be in there one at a time, okay?"

"Yes, that's fine," she replied, and disappeared beyond the pod's door.

Lucy did exactly as the guard said, and when she heard the click on the door, she entered the small interview room and took a seat on the steel stool. A large Plexiglas window separated her from the other side, and a few air holes were cut into it for whoever was on the other side to communicate.

She looked around at the inside of the small brick cubicle that they called an interview room, and for the first time in her life, realized that she was slightly claustrophobic. Things were closed in so tight that she stood to her feet.

"Oh my God!" She panicked, and started breathing short and quick breaths through puckered lips. "I wish they hurry up!" she said to herself about the guards taking their time bringing her clients to her. Then she tried to gather herself. She stopped thinking about the small room and started thinking about seeing Pretty E, and instantly her run-in with claustrophobia disappeared and was replaced with an overwhelming sense of relief. She was relieved because for the past three months she'd been away, the only thing she could do was think of Pretty E, and now she was about to see him.

"Why does he stay on my mind so much?" she asked herself, then concluded that it was probably the way she had left. She had taken the cowardly way out because she didn't have enough of a backbone to tell him face to face, so she put it down on paper. The only good thing about it though, was that he never got a chance to read it. Rasul was the one who read it. He had just received the letter himself yesterday, and when she questioned him on why he had just gotten around to calling her today when she left the letter over three months ago, he explained to her that it was the way she slid it under the door. It had gotten wedged between the floor and the doormat, and someone had just found it the other day. *Good!* she thought when he told her. *Now I can tell him how I feel face to face.*

She wanted to tell him how much she loved him. Tell him why she resigned from her job and became a lawyer. Tell him she was sorry for pressuring Hit-Man to go against his will. Tell him she was sorry for him committing suicide for what it was worth, and then tell him about the baby— their baby—the one she was carrying right now. Tell him that she wanted him to be a part of its life, but how, if he didn't want to, it was fine, because she was keeping it anyway.

Then the door on the other side clicked.

■■■■■■

Dog was just throwing the blunt roach into the toilet when the guard, Ms. Williams, called them over the speaker in their cell. "Dog and Pretty E, y'alls' lawyer is out here to see y'all," she said.

"Who?" they asked in unison.

"Y'alls' lawyer," she answered, and clicked the door. "Only one of y'all can come out at a time."

"Awight," they responded.

"You want to go out first?" Dog asked Pretty E, opening the door.

"Nah, you go," Pretty E said. "I'ma take a shit while you gone, feel me?"

"I feel you. Just make sure you put some water on that shit, 'cause last time, nigga, you had the room stinking like a mu'fucka!"

"Man, fuck you, nigga! What is shit supposed to smell like, nigga?"

"Not like that, nigga! You need to start drinking some water or some 'em," Dog replied, and Ms. Williams came over the intercom again.

"Will one of y'all come on? Damn! Y'all got this lady out pacing the floor and shit."

"A lady?"

"Yeah, a lady."

"Our lawyer is a man."

"Well, he must cross-dress then," she said. "'Cause this is damn sure a woman."

"Alright, here I come."

Dog walked out of the room in his sweat pants and shower shoes that he'd brought from the prison commissary yesterday, and the guard, Kareema Williams, smiled at him.

Bitches ain't shit! he thought, knowing she was digging him but fucking one of his workers. *I know what,* he said to himself, making a mental note. *If I get some time, I'ma knock her ass off.*

"You ready?" she asked him as he tucked in his T-shirt at the door.

"Yeah, I'm ready. Are you?" He smiled, grabbing the handle.

"Been ready!" she blushed, and clicked the door.

"We'll see," he said, and disappeared through the door when she clicked it.

Dog stepped into the small interview room, and the first thing he thought when he saw Lucy was that the Feds had stepped in and took over the case. Then he thought that maybe she was there to offer a deal to them, but that was definitely out of the question. "What da fuck you want?" he stated firmly, catching her off guard, but then she remembered that they didn't know she was no longer a federal agent.

"Michael, calm down. Just listen to me for a minute. I'm not the Feds anymore, I'm your attorney."

"My attorney?" he asked, baffled.

"Yes, your attorney. I took over today when I received the call from Rasul."

"Rasul?"

"Yes, Rasul," Lucy said, and went into the story.

Lucy started from the top. She explained everything to Dog, from the letter, clear down to the call she received from Rasul. The only thing she didn't reveal to Dog was her pregnancy; that part she decided was for Eric. She did tell him the good news though, the news about the new bail hearing she had gotten them for tomorrow morning, and he was more than happy. "So more then likely we'll get a bail tomorrow."

"Okay," he said.

"Okay, that will about do it then. Can you please tell Eric to come in now? And, uh, I'll see you in court tomorrow," she said, and Dog got up to leave.

When he got to his cell, he didn't say a word. The only thing he could do was shake his head. His mind was blown away, but at the same time, he was relieved. Lucy was an ex-cop. He knew she knew the law, and their chances of winning at their trial had just increased by ten percent.

"What happened, cousin? Who was it?" Pretty E asked.

"Man, this shit is about to fuck your head up, you heard me?"

"What?" Pretty E asked, thinking the worst case scenario.

"Man, just go see."

Pretty E bobbed out of his cell with the unusual bob in his step, and strolled over to the door next to the bubble.

The swagger in his step wasn't an act, it was really him. He was just that cool. He was the real life Rudy from the cartoon "Fat Albert". The only difference was that Rudy had no class, and Pretty E was full of class.

When the door clicked open and he walked through to the interview room and saw Lucy, he was at a total loss. One side of him was happy to see her, his lover, but the other side of him was filled with disgust. He couldn't believe that she had the audacity to even show her face to him, the way she betrayed him. She had lied to him. She was a federal agent that was doing undercover work on the Capelli crime family, and pulled him right into her madness. She was the reason one of his best friends was dead and the reason they were under a federal investigation, until they won their trial. They won because the State's star witness was dead; his best friend, Hit-Man. The only one that was convicted was Lenny (Fat Boy) Ionni before that, and he hadn't seen her since. The least she could have done was give him an explanation.

"What the fuck you want? Why are you even here? I hope you're not here to work no deal, 'cause you could've saved the trip!" he snapped.

"Eric!"

"Eric my ass! You got some muthafucking nerve! Guard! Guard, crack dis mu'fucking door so I can get da fuck up out of here!"

"No, Eric! Wait! Wait! Please, honey, don't leave!"

"Wait for what? I don't have anything to say to you," he said, and grabbed the door handle to leave.

"Eric, I'm pregnant!" The words escaped her mouth, and she instantly wanted them back.

"Pregnant?" he asked.

"Yes," she said, and lifted her shirt to show him her potbelly. "But that's not all. I love you! I loved you from the minute you walked into Lenny Fat Boy Ionni's construction sight, and baby, I'm sorry. I'm sorry for everything. But what I'm most sorry for is that I left without a word. That I wasn't a woman, and that I didn't come to you, Eric, and let you know who I was, how I was, and how much you changed me."

"I love you, sweetheart! You put a balance in my life, made me see things through your eyes, baby, so now I know. I know what you and your friends' side of life feels like. You were right, baby; *'Who Said Da Game Was Fair?'* Who ever said it, baby, was a liar, because now I know different. I know now, baby, that the bad guys aren't always the bad guys. I mean, for instance, take you guys. You guys had to sell drugs to make better livings for yourselves because of the living arraignments y'all were placed in, you know? I mean, Dog's mother was using, Hit-Man's mother was using, and even Rasul's mother was using before she got clean, but you were a different story. You didn't have to do what you did, but you did. That showed me the meaning of loyalty and friendship. You refused to turn you back on your friends and joined their struggle."

"So, was it wrong for you guys to survive under those conditions? No, I don't think so. Is it wrong that people have to steal and rob because they can't get a decent job to support their kids? No! So see, baby, that's what you gave me; the ability to look at everything from all sides instead of one-sided, do you understand?" she asked, having grabbed Pretty E's full attention.

"Yes, of course I understand. It's my life, but you say that to say what?"

"Baby, I say that to say I'm no longer a federal agent. I resigned from the job to become a defense attorney, and I've been doing great. I haven't lost a case yet, and I don't plan on losing this one either."

"This one?"

"Yeah, I'm your lawyer. Yours and Michael's. Rasul called me today, and I dropped everything and I came right here."

"How did Rasul find you? How'd he know that you were a lawyer?"

"Because I left a letter."

"A letter?"

"Yes, a letter. I left it under the club's office door before I left. I left it for you, but somehow it got lost. Whoever was sending him his mail to Florida just found it a few days ago, and he must have just gotten the letter today," she said, and he shook his head before changing the subject.

"So, what's this about you being pregnant?"

"I just found out today. I'm going to make a doctor's appointment tomorrow to see how far along I am."

"So, wha's up? What chu going to do? Are going to keep it or what?"

"Of course I'm keeping it! Why would I not?"

"No particular reason. I just wanted to know, that's all," he said before continuing. "So, where does that leave us?"

"I don't know, Eric. That leaves us wherever you want us to be. I love you. I do want you to be a part of the baby's life, but it's all up to you."

"I want to be a part of my child's life, and yours too for that matter, but we gotta work on some shit, you know?" Pretty E said, realizing just how much he really did care for Lucy.

The three-month escapade that they had gone on together had given them both a totally new experience. They explored the forbidden boundaries of interracial laws set by America, and understood for themselves why so many people before them had already crossed the boundary. They crossed because you couldn't control the way your heart felt. It was nothing to see a black man with a white woman, or a white man with a black woman in today's society, because the days of old had come and passed like last years calendar.

Pretty E and Lucy had grown into one another. They grew a bond between themselves, and the more he stared at her, the more he couldn't change the way he felt. Lucy was absolutely gorgeous physically, and her complexion, almost almond-like, gave her the look of a Hispanic woman, but her face was almost identical to Carmen Elecktra's.

"Why are you staring at me like that?"

"For no reason at all, baby… no reason at all." He laughed to himself, as he thought, *Damn, I got jungle fever like a mu'fucka!*

Chapter Three

Rasul's trip to Orlando, Florida had to end early because of some poor decision making on Dog and Pretty E's behalf. He explained to them before he left that Frankie gave word that the Feds were watching their every move, but they didn't listen. Now their choices had affected the way he and his family had to go about their free time together. That's why he had decided on this vacation anyway, because it would give him time away from the business side of his life, and time to focus in on his personal life. *Maybe it's just time for me to branch off,* he thought on more than one occasion because of situations just like this. He thought this way more regularly, now that he had a family, because they were first in his life today. He had a wife and a baby that was due any day now, a stepson who needed him around to set an example, and he had his freedom that he wanted to keep.

These were his priorities, but then there were his boys and the love he had for them. That love that ran deep into the marrow of his bones; the love that went beyond just a friendship and turned into more like a brotherly love. "How can I turn my back on them?" he asked himself as he thought about giving the life up. But the only thing that he could think of that was a good enough reason was Tameeka, Jaquaan, and the newborn he was waiting on.

Right then and there, Rasul knew he was done. The game was over for him. He just hoped his boys would feel the same way after their trial.

When the plane's wheels touched down in Philadelphia from Florida, the flight seemed a whole lot quicker than it did going down there. But all in all, it still took the four and a half hours needed for the trip.

He looked over at his wife who was awakened by the landing, then to his stepson who was gazing out of the window, and knew the decision he was making was the right one. *The game ain't fair,* he thought, and then his phone rang. "Hello!" he answered, as the plane sat parked on the runway.

"Hey, son! How're things going?" Frankie asked. "Are you enjoying your trip?"

"I was enjoying it, but I'm home now."

"Why did you leave so soon? I told you that I had everything under control with Dog and Pretty E."

"I know, Frankie, but I need to be there too, you understand? They are my brothers. They did eight straight with me, you can bear witness to that, so I have to be there for them now, you know?"

"I can understand that."

"So, how are you doing?"

"Oh, I'm fine I guess. How'd you like the beach house?"

"I loved the beach house. I didn't want to leave. I'm thinking about going back after Pretty E and Dog's trial, but you know what I've been thinking?" he asked.

"No, what's that?"

"I think you should let me have it," he joked.

"You want it?"

"Yeah, I want it," Rasul answered.

"Okay, it's yours. I'll leave it to you in my will, how about that?" Frankie said honestly.

"That's all good, but you're going to live forever. I might not ever get that, huh?"

"No, no, that's not true, Rasul. I'm not doing as well as you think."

"What? What's that supposed to mean?"

"Do you remember when I used to go to medication call when we were in the can?"

"Yeah, I remember."

"Well, that was for my prostate cancer."

"And?"

"And at my doctor's appointment today, he said it has regressed."

"So doesn't regress mean to leave or go back?"

"Yes, and it has come back"

"So what are you saying, Frankie?"

"I'm saying you're not always promised tomorrow, so take the bitter with the sweet. You have to live every day of your life like it's the last day of your life."

"I heard that!"

"Don't just hear it, take heed to it."

"I am."

"Good. So, how do you like the lawyer?"

"I didn't. I fired him today."

"Why'd you do that?"

"Because he couldn't even get a bail for them!"

"Probably because it is such a high profile case," Frankie said.

"Maybe so, but I still didn't feel right about going with that dude, you know? I just had this gut feeling."

"So, who did you hire?"

"Jennifer Vault."

When Frankie heard the name Jennifer Vault roll from Rasul's lips, a bitter taste filled his mouth. Jennifer Vault was Lucy, the federal agent who helped the prosecution gather enough evidence to land Lenny (Fat Boy) Ionni seventeen years in the Federal Penitentiary. She was the one who pressured that young guy, Hakeem, into giving up the tapes that would have given them all life sentences. She was the one who disappeared into thin air right before their trials. She was the one with the price on her head, the hundred thousand dollar price. She was the one who had to die!

"Jennifer Vault?" Frankie asked before continuing. "Are you losing your mind? The slut is a Fed! Do you understand what you are saying?" He didn't wait for an answer. "Don't you remember rule number one: Once a pig or rat, always a pig or rat?"

"Yes, Frankie. But the only reason that bail was denied was because of Detective Cohen. Lucy knows everything about that muthafucka. Plus, she loves the hell out of Pretty E. At least with her I know she's going to fight at trial." Rasul said, but Frankie didn't respond. "Are you there?" he asked.

"Yeah, I'm here. I'm just thinking, that's all," he responded, trying to figure out what decision to make next.

"Thinking about what?"

"Thinking about what to do with this Lucy broad, Rasul. Do you realize what you doing to me? You have me in between a rock and a hard spot. This is a woman who put Fat Boy in the can for seventeen years, and almost got us all life sentences. I've been busting everybody's balls in the Family to find this dame, and here she walks right back into the picture willingly. I have no other choice but to make this no good broad into fish food. Yeah, that's what I'll do. I'll chop her up and feed her to the fish. I just don't know whether to do it now or after the trial."

"After the trial, Frankie. Please! I really believe she can win the trial."

"Okay, Rasul. I'm going to do it for the sake of Dog and Pretty E's trial. But I swear to you, Rasul, after the trial, she's a dead woman!"

"Okay, Frankie. Whatever you say."

"I know it's what I say. I paid the cost to be the boss! She's a dead fuckin' woman!" Frankie said, and hung up the phone.

Rasul heard the anger in Frankie's voice before the phone went dead in his ear. He knew he had to be mad, because in all the years he knew Frankie, he never once cursed him or directed anger towards him. *Damn!* he thought, looking blankly into the dead phone as his wife stared at him as they walked through the airport.

"Wha's wrong, baby?" she asked, noticing the change that was evident on his face.

"Nothing. I'm alright," he lied.

Rasul wasn't alright though. Everything that he had done up to this point in his life, from the murders, to the dealing, to the suicide of his best friend and partner, Hit-Man, had his life in complete turmoil.

He closed his eyes and tried to shake free the thoughts that were haunting him, but all that did was make it worse. His thoughts were now becoming visions, and as they flashed through his head like movie clips, one particular one stood out. He tried to change it, the thought that became glued on pause, but it wouldn't leave. The dog was clamped down on her leg and shaking it while she screamed. Then there was the ambulance and the two paramedics, the ones who looked completely opposite but were twins, the wallet, her I.D., her beauty. His eyes snapped open and the images were gone. *Shelly!* he thought, as he remembered.

Tameeka knew something was wrong with her husband, but she couldn't put a finger on it. At first she thought that maybe it was because of the arrest of Dog and Pretty E, but that couldn't be it, she decided. His look was far too distant, like he was in deep concentration, in a place all by himself, and it began to worry her. She wanted to help him, but she didn't know where to start. *What could I do? I don't even know what was troubling him,* she thought, feeling helpless. *Damn!* she said to herself, and her instincts said grab his hand. She didn't know how it would help him, but she sure was sending him a message letting him know she had his back, and he must have got it, because he gave her hand a squeeze.

■■■■■■

The New Castle County Courthouse in Wilmington, Delaware, was the stage for one of the most talked about bail hearings in the State's recent history. Every news van from the Tri-State area was in attendance, and Lucy was pissed. *How the hell did this leak out so fast?* she wondered, because she just got the bail hearing last night. Whoever the culprit was, she wished she could get her hands around his or her neck to wring it, and wring it good. The news media was the last thing she needed in a trial like this, because the news media had a way of painting a picture that could change the outcome of a verdict with one flash of a bulb or one misquoted statement.

"There she is!" a news reporter yelled from beyond the media frenzy.

Lucy looked, and bulbs flashed like lightning before she actually knew what was going on. She was under the attack of raging media frenzy. *Oh my God!* she thought, and picked up her pace as she raced towards the courthouse.

"Ms. Vault! Ms. Vault!" they yelled from behind her as she made it into the safety of the courthouse... or so she thought.

Inside of the courthouse there was even more of a media circus going on. Reporters were everywhere. The hallways were clustered to a point where she had to brush her way through the chaos.

"No, I'm not answering any questions! No, not right now!" she answered, avoiding the media's questions.

"Is it true that you and Eric Benson are lovers?" a reporter blurted out, and Lucy's heart dropped.

"Aren't you the same federal agent that cut a deal with the deceased, Hakeem Stewart, to get Pretty E, also known as Eric Benson, and Dog, Michael Lollie, off of an indictment charge before?" another one asked.

"And what about their friend, Rasul Jefferies?" another one coat tailed off the question.

"Yeah, and what about their ties with the Mob?" another one asked. "Yeah, the Capelli Family?"

Lucy was horrified at the questions. She needed to make it into her new arena, the Superior Court room.

When she reached Courtroom 6-A, relief instantly overcame her, but she was still puzzled. How did they know those things? Why were they attacking her like this? *I'm not the one on trial. I'm the lawyer, for Christ sake!* she thought.

"I hate the media! I hate them!" she said underneath her breath as she thought back on what had just taken place moments ago. The nasty questions and crazy comments only fueled her fire to want to win even more. In fact, she *had* to win. She had to walk out of the courthouse today with her lover at her side, smiling into the cameras, and let them speculate some more. She yearned to feel him deep inside of her, needed to lick his sweat-soaked chest again. She needed to taste him, every inch of him. She needed him to make her legs shake, make her cum, needed to hear him moan her name through his big soft lips. Her panties were soaked.

■■■■■■

Detective Cohen was infuriated this morning when he got to work and saw the subpoena laying across his fax machine. "Who the fuck gave them a new bail hearing?" he asked himself as he snatched the paper from the machine. When he saw the Court Commissioner's name at the bottom, the only thing he could do was smirk. Commissioner Spacey was always the lenient one of all the commissioners, and the one the police department disliked the most because of his fairness. He treated even the worst of criminals with the utmost respect. His motto was, "They're innocent until proven guilty", so he knew why they were granted a new bail hearing.

The shit he and the prosecutor pulled yesterday should have never been allowed, but it was. *I guess when you do slick shit it really does come back to bite you on the ass!* he thought before reading on.

Cohen and the prosecutor both had pulled out all kinds of stunts to keep Pretty E and Dog behind bars. They even went as far as to bring things up that had nothing to do with the allegations to this case, but when he saw that they had the same judge, he smiled. "Shit, we'll just do it again," he said to himself as he picked up his phone.

Cohen called every news station in the Tri-State area and told them about the hearing today, making the same allegations as before. He knew what the power of the press could do, so he painted as nasty a picture as he could against the men he knew were responsible for his partner's death.

Now all he had to do was help the prosecutor get a conviction against them that would land them in jail long enough for him to build a case of murder against them for the death of his partner and mentor.

Cohen was ecstatic when he reached the courthouse and saw the media frenzy. Instead of avoiding them like Lucy did, he fed them, giving the media sharks all of the meat they could swallow down with their cameras, recorders, pens and paper, before heading into Courtroom 6-A.

■■■■■

Their court van pulled into the courthouse parking lot and headed into the garage. The reporters there to cover the story swarmed the van like a pack of wild hyenas. Their actions were totally animalistic as they pushed through each other, jammed microphones up to the side of the van, yelled, blurted out questions, and slipped and fell over one another, all trying to be first to get the meat of the story. The sounds of their voices blended together on one accord made the array of questions sound like the laughs of the dog-like animals.

Dog and Pretty E couldn't believe their eyes as they stared at the posse of reporters trying to get them on camera. They never thought in a million years that a case this petty could gain so much attention, because people got knocked off like this every day.

However, when they saw all the press and media crowded there to cover their case, fear overcame them. They knew how Delaware was when it came to drugs, because they had mandatory drug sentencing guidelines specifically for drug charges. They passed the law in 1991 called "Trafficking", a charge in which you received a mandatory sentence of three years for just an eight-ball of crack cocaine, which was just a little more than three grams of the chunky white gold.

Damn! They both thought the same thing. *We might not never see the streets again!*

The fear came because it was a known fact what Delaware does to people convicted on drug charges. There were plenty of 'hood legends that received long sentences for getting jammed up with lesser quantities than they had, but there was one that stood out to them the most. The one who pioneered the city for being the first young boy on his shit, and that was the boy from the 2-6 Projects, formally on 26th and Locust Street. Many had forgotten about the 18 year old prodigy who went down to the trafficking law in 1991 when he received a mandatory 44 year sentence. He was busted with a kilo and a half, a Tech 9, over thirty thousand dollars in cash, and an abundance of food stamps. The good thing about it though, was that due to a strong appeal, many people will see his face again, and all those who forgot will get to know the legend when he touches down in the next few years.

Dog and Pretty E weren't trying to have to go through all the appeal shit though. They wanted to spank the case on the first go around.

"Let's go! Come on, it's show time!" the guard driving the van said as he brought the truck to a stop inside the garage. "All those people are here to see y'all. Y'all are the stars of this show. I guess that drugs don't pay, huh?" the guard laughed as he helped them off of the van in shackles and handcuffs.

Dog ignored the comment, but made a mental to himself that no sooner than he was free and clear from all charges, he was going to make him pay for the smart remark. *Word on H-Town!* Dog was thought, swearing on his dead homie. *I'ma make that house nigga fertilizer for grass and daisies!*

Pretty E was thinking the same thing.

■■■■■■

Superior Courtroom 6-A was the stage, Judge Silverstone was the director, and the actors to this play on life were almost in position.

The D.A., Kevin Donavan, was a hungry young prosecutor aiming for a seat in office, and taking down whoever set out to challenge him in a courtroom. His conviction rate was well over 90 percent—more like 95 percent to be exact—but Lucy was looking to change that. She knew the prosecutor, Mr. Donavan, on a first name basis from her days as a federal agent. However, their bitter-sweet relationship had come to an abrupt end after she shot down one of his many attempts to get her into his bed.

When he looked over to his right at the defendants' table and saw Lucy, the woman he planned on building a future with, revenge filled his heart. The case was no longer a job he had to do; it was now personal. He would embarrass her in his victory, and then bask in her defeat as she became another victim in his on slate of convictions.

Lucy smiled when they made eye contact, remembering the many attempts he tried at getting her into his bed. She didn't know if he was still harboring ill feelings towards their past or not, but she was sure glad it was him prosecuting the case. *This is probably my only chance at making this a fair trial,* she thought, as instinct to save her lover kicked into high gear. Lucy batted her eyes seductively in an attempt to entice him with some old feelings she could use to her advantage in the case, but when he frowned, that plan flew straight out the window. *I guess I'm going to have to beat him fair and square,* she thought, then rolled her eyes.

■■■■■■

Detective Cohen stepped into Courtroom 6-A, dressed in jeans, a T-shirt, sneakers, a blazer, and his gun in a holster at his side in plain view. He was more then gratified at the turnout of people that filled the courtroom, because he was the State's main witness. He was also the officer who made the bust, and the officer who had become the talk of the town after making the arrest of two of the largest cocaine distributors in the entire Tri-State area. He had become a local hero to good, law-abiding citizens, and a shoe-in for the newly opened Commissioner of Police job that just became available, even if they lost the case. If they got a conviction, it was just icing on the cake.

"Detective Cohen!" a member of the press called out to him. "Can I have a minute, please?" he asked, but Cohen kept going. He didn't have time to talk right now. He needed to find a seat near the prosecution.

Lucy heard his name being called and turned around towards the murmur that grew louder upon his entrance. She stared into the crowd of people that gathered near the doors at the area of the courtroom, but couldn't find him amongst the many reporters. *Where is he?* she thought, and then he appeared out of the crowd, looking identical to the day they met at the hospital; tall and lanky. The only difference was that now he wore a five o'clock shadow that gave him a dirty look, and his pale skin was in need of deep tanning.

Then there were his eyes, the eyes that couldn't hide his thoughts or feelings because they didn't lie. The eyes showed everyone how he felt all the time, and this time was no different. There was some kind of deep hatred going on inside of him that was aimed directly at Dog and Pretty E, but Lucy couldn't put a finger on what was exactly causing the hatred.

Then it hit her. It was his partner, the one who got killed during a robbery. *That's why!* she thought. *He still thinks they did it!*

She took a sip of her water. *Ten Minutes 'til show time!* she thought, glancing down at her Donna Karan watch.

■■■■■

Dog and Pretty E were escorted from the thirteen-man cell called the Bullpen by six guards, and were led to the elevator. This was the basement part of the courthouse, the place closed off to the public, but wide open for offenders. Bound in shackles and handcuffs, they took the widest steps the leg irons would allow them, and with every step, there was a scraping of the chains against the floor. The sound that the chains made sent chills up their spines, and a deep-rooted hatred down into the depths of their very essence. It was the hatred that ran through each and every Black man who had to wear the chains and cuffs. The hatred ran through them spiritually, from the ghosts of their ancestors in slavery. It was a hatred for captivity, and oh how they missed their freedom right now!

When they boarded the elevator, they were told to lock into the little cage that separated the criminals from the guards. Within seconds, their stomachs did a small flip and the doors opened on the six floor.

"You ready, baby boy?" Dog asked in good sprits.

"Yeah, I'm ready," Pretty E assured him as they stepped off the elevator and were led into Courtroom 6-A.

Inside the courtroom, every single person was on the edge of their seats, awaiting the main characters in this play of life. The press had their pens, notepads, and recorders out and ready for the hearing to begin, while the police sketch artists sat behind their drawing tablets.

The prosecution and defense did last minute preparations on their game plans.

When the side door to the courtroom opened and they dragged their feet across the courtroom floor over to the defense table, the way they looked in the chains and cuffs gave off the look Lucy so desperately wanted to avoid. To her, the media, and everyone else in the courtroom, they were already guilty, and that's what she feared. She had to get them a bail, because if they went to trial in chains and cuffs, it would sure paint a picture of guilt in the minds of the jurors, she was sure of it.

"Hi, baby!" Lucy whispered in Pretty E's ear as they took their seats at the defense table. "Everything is going to be fine, okay?" she said as they settled in. "Hello, Michael!"

"Hi, Lucy! Wha's up?" Dog asked.

"Nothing much. Just ready to get you guys up outta here, that's all," she said, smiling confidently and giving Dog a sense of confidence also.

The bailiff stood beside the judge's bench, and with power and zeal in his voice said firmly, "All rise! The Honorable Judge Silverstone is presiding. Court is now in session!" and then stood off to the side.

Judge Silverstone stepped through the door leading from his chambers in his black robe. His hair was feathered neatly on the sides, his facial hairs were trimmed neatly, and his nose was sharp and pointed, almost eagle-like. His eyes were set closely together and they were a deep black, giving him an almost sinister look. He looked younger than his fifty plus years, but stern; stern enough to erase any optimism you had in your head for assurance, and replace it with a sense of uneasiness. He took his seat behind his bench in his huge leather swivel chair and looked out over the courtroom and said, "Good morning!"

"Good morning, Your Honor," the prosecutor and defense replied.

"Proceed, Mr. Donavan," he said.

"Your Honor, we're standing before you today less than twenty-four hours later, going over the same things we went over yesterday. I don't know what for, but I do know that yesterday we established good enough reason why these two defendants shouldn't be released on any kind of bail. They are known drug dealers who, best described by Detective Cohen, were terrorists to society."

"Your Honor, I object! Mr. Donavan is speculating," Lucy interjected.

"Your Honor, the only thing I'm saying is that these two men, Mr. Eric Benson and Mr. Michael Lollie, are where they belong according to the records before me, and what they have been charged with. If I may, Your Honor, I would like to call Detective Cohen to the bench."

Cohen took his seat on the bench.

Dog gritted his teeth so tightly together that they made a crunching sound as he visualized a bullet ripping through Cohen's skull, the same way it ripped through Detective Armstrong's skull when he pulled the trigger.

"Please state your name for the record," Mr. Donavan asked.

"My name is Detective Cohen."

"Hi, Detective!"

"Hello."

"Can you please tell the court why you don't think the defendants should be released on bail?"

"Because they are menaces to society—" he began before he was cut off.

"I object, Your Honor! Again, all speculation."

"Ms. Vault is absolutely right. Mr. Donavan, please re-direct your questions in a manner where the witness can answer with facts and not speculations," Judge Silverstone said, his remark putting a smile on Dog and Pretty E's faces.

Just the way Lucy was objecting was more than the alleged "best lawyer in the Sate of Delaware" had done yesterday. She was actually fighting.

"Your Honor, I think I've said enough. In fact, I'm sure I've said enough. Their records date back to their juvenile years, and they're charged with the same things now as they were back then. So, it's obvious that they are what their charges claim, just on a higher level. Your Honor, they're drug dealers!" Donavan said.

"Defense, your witness."

"Good morning, Your Honor," Lucy said gingerly, flashing a big bright smile.

"Hello, Detective! Long time," she said, but the remark hadn't registered on him yet. Her face looked familiar, but he wasn't sure where he had seen her before. He just watched the woman closely as she moved about the courtroom gracefully.

Lucy knew from the way he looked at her that he didn't remember who she was. *That was sure a change though,* she thought as she went into her proceedings. "Your Honor, I have no need for Detective Cohen. Would you please excuse him from the bench?" she asked, and was granted her request.

Lucy looked over her shoulder at Donavan as the detective left the witness stand. This was only a bail hearing, and she saw absolutely no reason to use him now. Her odd move by not cross examining puzzled the prosecution and the defendants, but Lucy was totally in control.

"Your Honor," she began, directing her attention back to the bench. "There's no need to draw this out or make such a big deal or circus over a bail hearing. My clients, Mr. Eric Benson and Mr. Michael Lollie, have been charged with a few felony offenses, yes, but the offenses are not capital murder. They do warrant a bail. That's why we're here today, because I'm not the only one who honors my Amendment rights. It seems as though the Court Commissioner does too. That's how we got a new bail hearing overnight," she continued, her sarcasm cutting to the core of Judge Silverstone.

He was the one who made the decision to deny the bail in the first place, and the remark sure wasn't going to help his decision today, he thought as he made a mental note of the comment.

"Your Honor, as for my clients' records, they have none as adults. All of their convictions are resulting from juvenile delinquents to young upstanding members of society. The decision to grant a bail should be quiet easy. First of all, my clients are lifelong residents of the State of Delaware. My clients own two prominent concrete businesses, landscaping businesses, and a nightclub that has become one of the best on the East Coast, and they're American citizens. Your Honor, please. Let's not waste the peoples' tax money any longer by keeping these two men in jail. Let's give them an opportunity at a fair trial by granting them a bail, because from the looks of these chains and cuffs binding my clients together, I've already come to a conclusion, as well as I'm sure the jurors will too," she finished and walked away.

The closing to Lucy's arguing statement was powerful and nearly borderline perfect. Her words had captivated the audience, and had nearly everyone in attendance nodding their heads in agreement. She turned towards her clients and flashed her pearly white smile before taking a seat at the defense table, as the Judge stared at the paper in front of him while rubbing his temple. He was trying to come up with a reasonable bail for them while sticking to the guidelines, but he remembered the mental note he had made from earlier.

"Can the defense and prosecution please stand?" Judge Silverstone said, giving Lucy and Donavan an awkward look as they stood.

"Stand up!" Lucy whispered to Pretty E before she stood, and in turn he tapped Dog and he stood also.

"I've taken into great consideration everything that the both of you said. I admit that the decision made yesterday was made prematurely, so today I'm going to amend it. I'm setting a trial date for December the 14th and a bail at one million dollars apiece," he said, enhancing the bail from the three hundred thousand dollar bail he was planning on giving them because of his mental note.

Detective Cohen and the prosecutor, Donavan, were pleased with the million dollar bond the judge handed out because they figured there was no way they'd make that kind of bail. They looked at each other, smiled, and then shook hands as they left the courtroom, still smiling as they passed the defense table.

Lucy, Dog, Pretty E, and Rasul were smiling too, but they were smiling because they were granted a bail. It wouldn't have mattered if the bail was two million apiece, they would have posted it.

When they were asked to stand and leave the courtroom, Lucy hugged them both. "We're going to post your bails right now," she assured them as they were led off.

Right before they disappeared behind the same door they entered through, Pretty E turned around. Lucy gave him a wink and a smile, and he responded with a smile and nod of his head and half-puckered lips, and her panties instantly became wet. *Mmm, mmm, mmm!* she thought. What she didn't know was that she caused a rise in him too!

"Come on, Lucy. Let's go pay these bails," Rasul said.

"Yes, please, please, *ple-e-e-e-ease* hurry up, 'cause I need my baby home!" she replied.

Damn, she gone! Rasul thought to himself as he burst out laughing at the thought of what pretty E had done to her. *Dat nigga probably ate her ass and everything!*

"What's funny?" she asked about the outburst.

"Nothing, just thinking, that's all… just thinking."

Chapter Four

Rasul walked up to his bank, Wachovia, with Lucy close in tow. They were escorted by two Wilmington police officers ordered to usher them to and from the sheriff's office due to the amount of money Rasul would be carrying back to the courthouse. Two hundred thousand dollars cash money was what he'd be lugging back in a briefcase; ten percent of the two million dollar bail he needed to pay. The Wachovia bank on 10th and King Street had already been notified by the main branch on Route 202 that he'd be coming, so when he arrived through the bank's front doors, the manager was already waiting.

"Hello, Mr. Jefferies," the manger, a tall young white girl fresh out of college greeted. "I've been waiting for you," she said, and led him into her office.

"Hello, how are you today?" he asked in response.

"I'm fine, Mr. Jefferies. How about you?"

"I'm fine, and you don't have to be so formal. You can call me Rasul."

"Okay, Rasul, and you can call me Ashley."

"Fine, Ashley."

"Here, have a seat. I'll be right back," she gestured and left the office.

Rasul looked around the small cubical made into an office, and observed his surroundings. He saw photos of her and her friends at a graduation on her desk, and photos of what he guessed to be her family next to them, then wondered what his life would have been like had he and his boys done the same. Probably stress-free, he imagined, turning his attention to the small square trashcan on the side of her desk. Rasul let his eyes roam through the contents of her trash, because he knew from experience that you could tell a lot about a person by what was in it, and Ashley was a health food nut.

Ashley walked back into the office carrying a briefcase with a lock on it, and said, "I'm sorry to keep you waiting," then flopped down in her chair.

"No need to apologize. I have plenty of time," he assured her.

"Well, let's get started then," she said, and flipped open the briefcase. She grabbed one of the stacks of money from the briefcase, licked her fingertips, and started to count. She did it all by hand because she couldn't afford for the bill counter to make a mistake. Two hundred thousand dollars was just too much money to have to keep counting over and over again, so she did it manually. It was the best way, she decided. She counted each of the individual money stacks that contained ten thousand per stack, and then passed it to Rasul, who counted it again. Within the next thirty-five minutes, they had twenty stacks of money equaling two hundred thousand dollars.

Ashley placed the money neatly back into the briefcase and thought to herself, *How did this young man get all this money?* This wasn't the biggest money transaction she had ever done, so she didn't make a big issue about it. She just thought it to be strange that such a young man, and a Black one at that, would have so much money and not be someone famous like a professional athlete or something.

"Will that be all?" she asked.

"Yes, that'll be all," Rasul replied, and stood up to leave.

Rasul came walking from behind the office cubicle, carrying the briefcase, and Lucy immediately relaxed. Her anxiety had taken over completely as she stood with her arms folded while tapping her foot, but now she was relieved. The idea of her being held in her lover's arms wasn't an idea anymore, it was reality.

"Is everything okay?" she asked.

"Yeah, everything is cool. Now, let's go get my peoples out of there!" he responded as the police escorted them back to the sheriff's office.

■■■■■■

"*...They took off my shackles,*
Let me out the hole,
Ate my last soup,
Took off my prison clothes,
Took the handcuffs from around my wrists.
Can't believe freedom's on the other side of the
fence..."

Oschino
"Best of Oschino Vol. 1"
"The Roc"

Pretty E and Dog were called up to the bubble by the guard right before the shift changed, and were told bag the baggage.

"About time!" Dog said, and didn't waste any time heading back to his cell. "Yo! Crack nineteen!" he said as he stood at the door holding the handle and one hand in the air.

"Wha's up, Pretty E? Y'all out of here?" a dude named Kevin asked.

"Yeah, we out of here, my nigga," Pretty E said, and gave him the right hand followed by a half-hug.

"Dat's wha's up!" he replied before asking, "Wha's up? Can I get those?"

"Damn right you can have these muthafuckas," he said, stepping out of the white Air Ones with the blue swoosh sign. "You know you gotta give me *them* though," Pretty E said, talking about the State sneakers.

"I know, 'cause they won't let you leave in shower shoes no more. They on some dumb shit. They don't even want to let a nigga leave his sneakers behind to a mu'fucka. These guards are petty as hell," Kevin said as they made the trade.

"I know that's because the muthafuckas that work here are so miserable at themselves and the life they're living that they take their sick shit out on us. Feel me? Try to make our already fucked up situation worse. It's probably because they the same mu'fuckas that used to carry niggas like me book bags, you know?" Pretty E said, and they shared a laugh.

"I heard that!" Kevin said.

"Look, cousin, let me go. I gotta go pack my shit up so I can bounce," Pretty E said, and trotted off.

Dog threw everything the State issued to him in his pillowcase and tied it up just like the guard said. His personal things, like commissary, books, and hygiene, he gave away to the people he knew and the ones he just met.

His boy, Mark though, was his young boy, the one he played chess with every day and the one he really looked out for. Mark was his young gunner. He reminded Dog of himself in more ways than one, but what really stuck out to him most was his heart. "Young Gunner!" he called out for Mark.

"Wha's up, cousin?" he asked.

"Come in and shut the door for a minute," Dog replied, and Mark went in.

"Wha's up, Dog?" he asked as he pulled the door to a crack behind him.

"Here, baby boy. I got some 'em for you," Dog said, and passed him the cell phone. "Look, call me later on tonight so I can get all of your information and shit. I'm going to grab a lawyer up for you. Plus, I'ma send you some change so you can go to commissary. Here, take these too," he said, and handed him the extra batteries.

"Thanks, cousin," Mark said, and then continued. "Yo, if you get me the lawyer before my preliminary hearing, the judge will probably throw that shit out. How they going to charge me with an attempted murder or gun charge when there ain't no gun or witnesses? Feel me?"

"I feel you, baby. That's why I'ma get right on it. I need you home with me, baby boy, 'cause I got a lot of shit for you to do, you heard me?"

"Yeah, I here you loud and clear," he replied as the door swung open.

"Yo, nigga! Is you ready to get da fuck up outta here?" Pretty E asked all hyped up.

"I've been ready, nigga. You the one that ain't ready," Dog replied.

"You a lying ass too," Pretty E said, and threw everything the State gave him onto his bed. In one swift motion, he tied everything up in the sheet and said, "Why ain't I ready?" and they all laughed like crazy.

"Yo, nigga, you crazy as hell!" Dog said.

"Dog, did you give 'im the trees and shit?" Pretty E asked.

"Oh shit, I forgot all about the trees! I did give him the phone though," Dog Said, and he got down on his hands and knees to reach up under his bunk. When he stood back up, he held in his hand the weed he had taped up there last night. "Here, cousin, and don't get caught with this shit," he said, passing the weed, lighter and blunts to Mark.

"I ain't," he said as the guard interrupted their little get-together by shouting over the intercom.

"Benson! Lollie! Do y'all want to leave?"

"Yeah, we want to leave!" they said in unison.

"Well y'all better come on then, 'cause y'all's ride is here to take y'all down to booking. So if y'all don't want to get caught up in the shift change, y'all better come on or y'all will be caught up 'til after dinner," he said, and that's all they needed to hear.

Dog and Pretty E were out of there.

■■■■■■

Outside of the prison, Lucy sat parked behind Rasul, impatiently waiting for Pretty E and Dog to be released. She flipped down her sun visor to look in its mirror, but they weren't there. Her Marlboro Lights were on I-95 probably smashed to pieces by now, but she sure could have used one right now. She needed something to take her mind off of the wait, because her desire to see him was driving her crazy. She was yearning for him, literally. Shaking, she didn't know if it was the withdrawal from the nicotine, or whether she just missed Pretty E that much. Before last night it had been three whole months since she had last seen him, but she found out firsthand that her feelings for him were the same, if not stronger. Lucy felt the same way she felt for Pretty E as she did the time she first met him at Us Guys construction site;

giddy as a high school girl with a crush on the star quarterback.

Lucy looked into the mirror on her visor and noticed that she was glowing. Her face was full of color, and there was a noticeable weight gain around her cheeks and neck area. She knew the weight gain was from the baby, but where the glow and shine was coming from was unknown. "Damn, does he make me fell this good?" she asked herself, blushing for no reason.

She reached in her purse, grabbed her makeup kit and powdered her nose. "They should be out of there any minute now," she spoke to herself as she tried to look perfect for when Pretty E was finally released to her. "There!" she said, satisfied with her appearance, and closed the makeup kit and put it back in her purse "Perfect!"

■■■■■■

Rasul was growing tired of the wait, but knew it would soon be over. The Records Department inside of the prison had a way of playing with your paperwork when it came time for your release, but they were always on time when they sent you your sentencing orders or status sheets.

Rasul looked over at the huge brick building surrounded by razor wire and steel fences, remembering. He remembered all the birthdays, holidays, and New Years he had spent behind the steel doors. He remembered all the many laps he walked around the federal prison yard, the cries of young boys and men too weak to fend for themselves while they were being turned into some lifer's bitch. He remembered the sound of toothbrushes being scraped against the concrete floors as the handles where being sharpened into shanks for protection. Lastly, he remembered just how much he never wanted to see the inside of any more jail walls. The eight year sentence he had served was way more than enough jail time for him. He vowed to himself a long time ago that if he ever got into another jam, he was holding court in the streets.

Rasul looked through his rear view mirror at Lucy, who was applying makeup to her face. He began to feel guilty, because he was holding onto a secret that had enough magnitude to tear a person's soul apart; a secret that to hold on to, you had to be a cold-hearted person. But Rasul was not that person. It was eating at his conscience every second of the day having to hold on to something like this, but he was standing firm… for now anyway.

The weight of knowing that the person you called on to come help you was a walking dead woman could eventually break you down, but Rasul blocked it out. The thing that kept bringing it up was the phone call, though.

"Okay, Rasul," Frankie had said. *"I'll do it for Dog and Pretty E's sake, but I swear to you, after the trial she's a dead woman!"*

Those words continued to echo in his head no matter how hard he tried to block them out. That's what was making it rough, but he was doing well.

He thought back to just last week when everything was fine, and saw how dramatically life had changed for him in just seven days. The past six months were crazy as hell, from the death of his best friend, Hit-Man, to the arrest of his two remaining best friends.

The vacation was just what the doctor ordered. He needed it to make the decision that he made because it took his mind off of everything and everybody. The decision to give it all up was final; he just hoped Dog and Pretty E would be in agreement when he broke the news to them.

■■■■■■

Dog and Pretty E were led down to Booking and Receiving by a guard assigned to escort inmates throughout the prison hallways. That was what the guard on the tier meant by saying to them that their ride was there. Their ride, or their "Rover", was just another way of saying the guard was there to get them. It really didn't make a difference to theme either way what they called them, as long as they were there to get them so they could leave this place they called "home" for the past three days.

When they reached the Booking and Receiving part of the prison, all eyes were on them as they rounded the corner. Each and every guard, nurse, and inmate down in the area had locked their eyes in on them. It was a very rare sight to see someone make a million dollars bail, but they had posted the bond within hours.

"Wha's up? Where y'all want me to put this shit at?" Dog asked the shift commander seated behind the desk.

"Over there," he pointed, never lifting his eyes off the computer screen.

"Then what?"

"Then, go into that room over there and wait until we call for you," he said flatly.

Dog and Pretty E tossed their pillowcases into the laundry cart and did exactly what the guard asked them to do. They didn't respond to how flatly the shift commander spoke to them, because they were ready to leave. They couldn't afford to get on these people's bad side. They knew that if they had just the smallest confrontation with the guards, that the prison could legally keep them until midnight, even if their bails were paid, because it wasn't a new day until then.

Pretty E walked into the holding cell and took a seat on the bench, but Dog stood up and stared out of the window. This whole experience for him, from the moment they were arrested clear up to them fighting to get a bail for their freedom, had brought him back to reality. It snatched the cold right from his eyes, but failed to put any fear into his heart. Yes, he missed his wifey and the kids, but money still had to be made. This whole ordeal meant nothing to him. It only let him know that he wasn't untouchable, and that he had truly fallen asleep. He got too comfortable in the way the operations were moving and forgot to cover his back door. That was what was eating at him the most, he fact that he had lunched. There was no way in hell that he or Pretty E should have been anywhere near the drugs. They had workers for that. What he did know though, was that it would never happen again. "I mean that!" he said to himself.

Pretty E, on the other hand, was stuck on an emotional roller-coaster ride between two women, a nigga's quickest downfall. Not because they're women, because it took the focus off of what he was trying to do. That's what that meant. It didn't mean that a woman was a man's downfall, because in all reality, a man will only go as far as the woman behind him will take him. It just meant that Pretty E was allowing Tammy and Lucy to occupy too much of his time and thoughts, taking his mind off of what he had to do.

Now, as he sat there on the steel bench reflecting back to the day of the arrest, he realized that even then his mind was stuck on Lucy and the way she left or where she was going. She just up and disappeared. He didn't find out until Lenny Fat Boy Ionni's trial that she was actually the federal agent who had built a case against them all.

However, even then it didn't change the way he felt about her. She had shown him how to love by just loving him. No other woman had actually done that before. It was always just a fuck thing or what they could get from one another. It was never a love thing. The only one who came even close to making it a love thing besides Lucy was Tammy. However, he still had his thoughts about her too. He knew that she loved him, but to what extent, he questioned. But he knew he would have to make a decision real soon. It was time to get honest.

Lucy already knew about Tammy from her Fed days when she trailed the Lexus Coupe with the license that read "Pretty 1". He knew that, but Tammy had no clue. It was time to tell her about Lucy, because how was he going to explain a baby? Plus, this will show him where their love really stands.

"Wha's up, nigga? You a'ight?" Dog asked, noticing Pretty E staring out into space.

"Yeah, I'm a'ight," Pretty E answered as a guard rounded the corner carrying paperwork.

"Damn, I hope this is us, cousin!" Dog said, and hit the nail on the head, because the guard yelled out, "Benson, and Lollie! Come on!"

Chapter Five

When Rasul told me and Dog that he was done with the game, I couldn't my ears. I thought to myself like, *Damn, wha's up with him?* Then I remembered that I had a family now. He wasn't just my boy who became more like a brother to me over the years, he was a husband and a father, and I respect that. Maybe I need to go and contemplate on what he said some more, because on some real shit, the thought of chilling had crossed my mind too. Besides, he had come a long way from Clifton Park Projects and food stamps. I remember those days like yesterday, and the memories weren't sweet. The crazy thing about it all though, was that I didn't even have to hustle. My mom and dad are rich, but seeing my boys struggle so much, I preferred to struggle too. That's just because that's how much I value the term of friendship.

I remember when Christmas would come around, I'd tell my mom and dad that instead of buying me a whole bunch of gifts, just buy me the main gift four times so I could give each of my boys one, then we'd all have one. Like the Christmas when Nintendo came out, instead of me just getting one, we all got one. Those were the good old days, and my peoples were proud of me. They were happy that they raised a son who wasn't selfish, and cared about someone other than himself.

I looked over at Lucy as I lay back in the passenger seat of her Maximum, and didn't say one word. I could tell she was feeling uneasy by the way I got in the car and responded to her big and bright smile like, *Hey, wha's up?* I was still mad at her for the way she left, but as I stared at her fine ass, I was sure glad she was back. I would never tell her that though, because then I'd be carrying my heart around on my shoulder. I wanted her to sweat a little bit more first. I wanted her to apologize again and again, make me feel like she was in debt or some 'em, because that would keep her at distance for a while, and give me enough time to explain to Tammy the jam I had gotten myself into. If she doesn't except the fact that Lucy is having my baby, then she gotta go. This is my first child, and I'll be damned if some woman comes between it and me. I love Tammy to death, but my child is a part of me. If she makes me decide, the comparison is none.

"Pretty E," Lucy called out to him.

"What?" I answered bluntly.

"Can you please say something to me? Your silence is killing me."

"What chu want me to say?" I shot back at her, trying to cut the conversation short, but she hit me with some shit that almost worked until I flipped it on her.

"You could al least say thanks."

"Say thanks?" I couldn't believe she said that shit. I looked her dead in the eyes before going on and said, "You got some motherfuckin' nerve! Why should I say thanks for some shit that you supposed to do? Shit, you owe me this, don't you? The least you could do, since you just disappeared with no explanation, is defend me, right? After all, you got me caught up in this bullshit anyway."

"What do you mean I got you caught up in this mess?" she asked.

My words must have cut her deep, because tears welled up in her eyes. I said, "Had your sorry ass told me you were a cop, I would have never fucked with your ass! I would have stayed as far away from Us Guys Construction as possible, and then you would have just had your case against the Mob. You wouldn't have had any reason to follow behind us, investigating and shit. That's why the police started following me, because before you came along, the police didn't even know my name. Then on top of that, if it wasn't for you, my boy would probably still be living!" he shouted out, trying to hurt her, and it worked, because tears were every where.

"I'm sorry! How many times do I have to say it?" she screamed, but I acted like I didn't give a fuck. I was working on my game plan to keep both of my women.

▪▪▪▪▪▪

I knew something was wrong the minute Eric got into my car. He was nowhere near as excited as I was about him coming home from jail, but I didn't say anything. I just smiled. At first I thought that maybe it was something that Rasul had said to him in the car with Dog, before he got into mine and they pulled off. Maybe it wasn't. All I know was that just having my baby next to me put me on cloud nine.

I wanted to say something badly, but decided against it. I didn't want to chance him taking out his frustration on me, because when he snapped on me yesterday at the prison, I was shocked. I never knew he could be so mean, as sweet as he was to me all the time. I knew one thing though; those were his true colors, because his words carried conviction. That was who Eric really was, so why was he so nice to me? Is it an act, or does he really like me like that? Who knows? I knew the job was rough before I took it.

I glanced over at Eric first, but he paid me no mind, so I turned up the radio. It's funny because he didn't say anything like, "Turn dat bullshit off!" When I turned up one of my favorite songs, "Hot Legs" by Rod Stewart, and then sang along with Rod for the entire song, he still didn't say anything.

I gathered myself, built up my courage, and then cleared my throat before saying, "Can you please say something to me? Your silence is killing me!" And just what I wanted so badly not to happen, happened anyway. Eric totally lost it on me, but I didn't say a word. I just listened with my mouth shut as he verbally bashed me. I tried to put myself in his shoes to see things his way, but I couldn't, because I viewed myself differently. I knew that by running off the way that I did was wrong, but I at least thought that by me coming back to help would ease any ill feelings. Oh, how so wrong I was! I couldn't do anything but cry, because I knew I hurt him, but I was sure going to make it up to him.

■■■■■■

I told Lucy not to go to the hotel, because I had been staying at the old apartment me and Hit-Man had down in Fox Run. I had decided that since I spent the majority of my time here in Delaware and usually didn't leave until late, I might as well keep the spot. Sometimes I wasn't done handling business or smutting something out until around two or three in the morning, and making that Philly ride up to Tammy's was not some 'em I was always trying to do. Besides, a nigga needs his own shit to call his own.

The house I had in Saddlebrook I rented out to Section 8, so the two-bedroom apartment was doing me fine. I had plans on buying a house with Tammy when I got out of jail, but I never knew this shit was going to happen. Now I had to deal with this bitch just poppin' up. Nah, I ain't going to call her no bitch, but damn, how she just going to pop up out the blue?

I put the key in the door to the apartment, stepped in, and immediately punched the code in on the alarm system. Yeah, niggaz, my shit was laid like that. I didn't have too much, just a little forty-two inch plasma flat screen looking like a picture on the wall. No more leather furniture, just a plush fabric sectional on some grown man shit, and a few pieces of art I bought up in Philly from Brother Hanif's on 832 South Street.

I turned to see the expression on Lucy's face, and just like I thought, she was mesmerized by my blackness and pleased with her surroundings. "It sure beats the hotel, huh?" I asked her, and she followed me into the crib.

"Are you hungry or some 'um?" I asked her.

"Yeah, why? What you going to do for me, cook or some 'em?" she asked me, wanting to see what I would say, and to her surprise I said, "Yeah, what chu want?"

■■■■■■

I really didn't know what I wanted, because I had been eating real crazy lately. Being pregnant was crazy, because my diet went straight out of the window. I was eating shit I hadn't eaten in years, so I needed to go look and see for myself what he had out there before I decided on what I wanted.

I looked through the cabinets first, but nothing caught my eye except some tomato soup. Then I looked into the refrigerator, and my eyes made my stomach want what it saw. I said, "Here, Eric, make this for me," and handed him the cheese, butter, bread, and tomato soup. "I want grilled cheese and some tomato soup."

He looked at me like I was crazy, and asked me was I serious. I responded with, "As a heart attack!" and then walked out to the living room and flopped down on the sectional. I grabbed the remote control and turned the TV to my new favorite channel, Lifetime, and to my surprise, they had a special on childbirth.

I said, "Eric, bring me some water!" and threw my feet up on the couch and got comfortable as I smelled the aroma from the butter melting in the pan out in the kitchen.

When I was finished eating, I was ready for some loving. I had a fire burning between my legs that only Eric's water hose could extinguish. I set my plate down on the coffee table and lay back in Eric's lap. My head was right on his dick, and I knew this is going to sound crazy, but I felt his dick getting hard against my jaw. That only made my pussy get even more soaked than it already was.

I turned around on my back so I could look him straight in the eyes, and he answered my question without even opening his mouth. He just slanted his eyes and licked his lips, so I knew what it was.

I rolled back over to my side, this time facing his crotch instead of the TV, and fidgeted with his pants. I got them open and he raised up just enough so I could get them down around his ankles, and he stepped out of them while he was still sitting down.

He was sitting on the couch, stark naked from the waist down, and I started my tricks, the ones I learned from my college roommates. I kissed his balls first, not too hard, just real tenderly, before placing them in my hands. He jumped when I grabbed them, but I didn't know what for, because I was being as gentle as I could. They say that balls are the most tender things in the world, and I knew that. So just to let him know that we were on the same page, I kissed them again, and then licked them on both sides before moving on.

I grabbed his dick and, oh my God! It seemed like it had grown since the last time I saw it. *Mmm, mmm, mmm!* I said to myself as I put it in my mouth. Still holding on to his balls, I went down on it and felt it growing inside my mouth. Up and down I went until I almost choked on it, then I slowed down.

"Damn, baby!" I heard him say, but I didn't respond. I just looked up at him while he was still in my mouth and moaned softly.

When he looked away from me, I knew he was under my spell. My plan was to make him forget that he was ever mad at me as I tried to suck the anger right out of him. He grabbed me on both sides of my head and pulled me down on all that dick by my hair, and squirted in my mouth. I swallowed each and every drop of his love juices and kept on sucking, because I refused to let his dick go down in my mouth. I was determined to keep it standing up strong as I unzipped my skirt.

Eric tugged at the buttons on my blouse until my cleavage-cut bra by Victoria's Secret stuck out from beyond the shirt's fabric. I knew he was pleased with my newfound titties that had grown overnight by being pregnant because of the way he caressed them. They were big and perfectly round to perfection, like I had gotten implants.

I stood in front of him and got ass hole naked and looked down at my potbelly, and he smiled. He reached out and ran his finger on the deep dark line that developed from my navel down to my hairline, then put his tongue where the line disappeared and tasted me. I put my foot up on the couch and stood there, holding him by the head as his tongue penetrated the lips of my forbidden fruit.

"Ooooh, baby!" I cried out as the sensations I was feeling escaped my mouth. "Baby, I'm sorry!" I cried. "Please baby, accept my apology. I love you!" I tried to convince him, but he knew I did.

Then I had to hold on to his ears tightly because I almost lost my balance as I came while standing up.

■■■■■■

Lucy lay her head back in my lap, and almost instantly my dick started getting hard. I tried to take my mind off of fucking or getting my dick sucked, but it had been a whole three days since I busted a nut.

"Fuck it!" I told myself as I felt my man rise. I knew she felt it too, because she started moving around before she finally turned over on her back and looked me straight in the eyes. I stared back in her eyes, but slanted mine a little bit before I licked my lips and lay my head back on the back of the couch.

She unbuttoned my pants, zipped down the zipper, and grabbed my balls as I kicked my pants the rest of the way off. I jumped like a muthafucka when she grabbed my balls though. I had to, because you know how tender balls are. I wanted to make sure that we were on the same page. To let me know she understood my message, she kissed them, and then licked them softly before putting my dick in her mouth.

"Damn, baby!" I said, sucking air through my teeth as she gave me some more of that wonder head. The way she worked her hands and mouth together was like magic. It was crazy, because the way she gave me head was like she enjoyed the act more then I did. That's what I loved about Lucy. Everything she did was done to prove that she loved me.

I closed my eyes for a second, but when I opened them and looked down at her, she was looking me straight in the eyes. If you never had that done to you before, you need to, because that shit is sexy as hell.

The next thing I knew, I was cumming like a muthafucka, and Lucy was swallowing every last drop of my shit. *Damn, she nasty as a muthafucka!* I thought, but I loved it. The only other time I could get my shit sucked like this was when I was paying a bitch, because sistas would suck it, but they told you straight up front, "Tell me when you about to cum, boy, for real. Don't cum in my mouth!" And they'd wonder why we cheat and go to the strippers.

After I got his nut off, I was cool. I thought it was going to be over, but Lucy didn't stop. Usually my dick would go down after my first nut, but for some reason it stayed up. My interest didn't go away or anything. I guess it was because Lucy looked so damn sexy while she continued on with my head job. Plus, I couldn't do anything but envision my dick slammin' in and out of her tiny pink pussy. Just on that thought alone, my dick got hard as a brick.

I stood up and turned her around with my chest up against her back and kissed her neck as she lay her head back against my shoulder. I used my hands to explore her every curve, and just like that, I remembered her skin was smooth and silky.

"Mmm!" she moaned, and reached back to grab my dick. "Put it in!" she begged, and I bent her ass over. I used my hand to reach under her and feel for that tight box, and grabbed my man with the other hand, while my first hand parted her lips.

"Grab your ankles," I said, and slammed all nine inches of my meat in her back. Nah, I'm bullshittin'! I only go eight and a quarter, but it still filled her up as she screamed a scream of pleasure, not pain.

Chapter Six

I don't know about Pretty E, but I was ready to get home. I had to see my wife and kids ASAP. The three days I had just spent in jail waiting on a bail were the longest I'd ever been away from my babies.

When Rasul first started talking to me and Pretty E, we looked at each other and kind of gave one another the look that said, "Yo, dis nigga is trippin'!" because it wasn't just something he was going through like we had thought. Rasul was dead serious about really getting out of the game. I wasn't trying to hear it, but the more he talked, the more sense he started to make. He was making a valid point.

We were the owners of some very prominent and profitable business venues, and we were millionaires, and we were getting older. There really wasn't a need to continue doing wrong, but that was all we knew, and really, the only thing we liked doing.

Another thing was that I always was a firm believer in the only thing that was better than what you had was having a little more that what you had. So, what was better than a million? Your absolute everything in life. I was the "can't stop, won't stop" type of nigga, and always was, you know?

I remembered back in the Clifton Park days when we were young bucks. I was the one who first started really stacking paper—well the second one—because Rasul was the same way.

Hit-Man was the one, though, who put us on from jump street, but he bullied his way to the top. If shit ain't go his way when we were younger, he would just take it, and that shit rubbed off on us. Hit-Man was the one who said, "Fuck this hustling shit, man. That shit is too risky. Why should we stand on the block all day pumpin' when we can just take dat shit, you know? Take dat shit and then sell it back to them." He would say that every day until we did our first stick up. Damn, I miss my boy, Hit!

But when Rasul came home, he was different. I mean don't get it twisted, he was still hard to the core. The type of nigga who would pop your top like a Crystal bottle at the drop of a dime. He just was on a different level than we were.

The eight year bid had groomed him well beyond his twenty three years, so maybe the rumor was true about jail making men out of boys. That was the good thing about him and his change up, because it kept us all balanced. When we was acting off of instinct and not thinking clearly, that nigga was focused. He had a vision and a plan that he laid out to all of us, one that would make us all millionaires and businesses owners in two years, and he made that shit come true. That's why when we listened to him talk, I knew he was right about what he was saying about giving the game up, but I wasn't trying to hear it. I just wasn't trying to give the game up right now, because I still got a rush for the lifestyle.

When we pulled up in front of my house, I saw my wife's Benz Wagon in the driveway. I told Rasul I would call him later and got out of the car and headed up the walkway.

Kim didn't know I was coming home, because I didn't tell her last night after Lucy popped up as my new lawyer. I didn't want to get her hopes up high on me coming home, and then they deny my bail again, so I decided to keep the good news to myself.

I reached in my pocket and grabbed everything out of it because I couldn't single out my keys alone. I had all kinds of shit in my pockets, from Chap Stick, bubble gum and paperwork, clear down to my shoestrings, and they were there because of the police. I was too lazy to put them back in my sneakers when the guard in Booking and Receiving handed me my personals in a small plastic bag, so I put them in my pocket along with the rest of the shit.

I was still trying to get some logic out of why they take your shoestrings when you get arrested anyway. The police say it's because people sometimes hung themselves with them, and I thought, so what? That doesn't mean everybody will. They should do mental health evaluations when you first get arrested instead, but they don't think that way.

I turned the key in the lock on the front door and stepped inside the house, and the feeling was unreal. I felt like just collapsing in the middle of the living room floor.

"Daddy! Daddy! Daddy!" my baby girl, Shakira, screamed as she ran full speed towards me.

"Yo, Mom! Daddy's here!" Rasul yelled. He was the middle boy, the one I named after Rasul when he was locked up. Then my favorite child came out, my spitting image, Little Mike. He wasn't my favorite child in the sense of I loved him any more than the rest of them, he was just my first born, my "Li'l Man", you know?

"Hey, baby girl! How's daddy's baby doing?" I asked and reached down to pick my "Li'l Princess" up.

Kim couldn't have heard all the noise the kids and I were making because she would have been running down the stairs. I guessed the shower water running and the stereo in my room that was turned up overrode all of the chaos the kids and I were making downstairs, but that was a good thing, because I wanted to surprise her anyway.

"Li'l Mike, how long has your mom been in the shower?" I asked.

"She just got in there, Dad."

"Alright, look y'all. I need y'all to be quiet for Daddy, okay? Daddy wants to surprise y'all's mom."

"Ok, Daddy," they all answered, giggling and laughing at the thought of making their mom happy.

"Okay, y'all. Stay down here and I'll be back after I surprise y'all's mommy, okay?" I said, and put Shakira down.

Since my son said Kim just got in the shower, I had time to go out into the kitchen to see what she was cooking that smelled so good. She was the best cook I'd ever seen, seriously, and I was not saying that because she was my wife either. She wasn't afraid to try something new every time she stood in the kitchen, and every time she experimented, it turned out to be delicious.

When I looked in the oven at her invention of the day, I saw skinless chicken breasts smothered in barbecue sauce, with sliced apples and oranges on top and a coating of honey. My mouth watered so bad that drool nearly dripped out of it, but I was able to slurp it up before that happened. The chicken looked so good that I started to pick up one of the breasts, but decided not to. I'd rather eat with my family.

As I walked up the stairs, I could smell the liquid soap my wife used. It was made by Victoria's Secret, and it had a tropical smell. I told myself that on a hungry day, its smell would probably tempt you to taste it, and I knew that's why she used it.

I stepped into the master bedroom, walked over to the adjoining bathroom door and turned the knob. To my disappointment, it was locked so I knocked.

"Who is it?" she asked, and then continued. "Damn! I can't even take a muthafuckin' shower with out y'all all up my ass!"

I didn't answer her. I knew Kim like a book, and knew that if I kept knocking she'd just snatch the door open, so I continued to knock. Just like I thought, she damn near yanked the door of the hinges.

"What! Got-damn it!" she snapped, thinking it was one of the kids.

"Hey, baby!" I said, and reached out to her, and she jumped in my arms, still soapy.

"Oh my God, baby! When did you get home?" she asked.

"Just now," I said.

"How did you get out?"

"Look, just go and rinse the rest of that soap off first, then we'll talk about it, okay?"

"Hell no!" she said. "I ain't getting in there by myself! You better come on!"

"Okay, okay, here I come," I said, and started to undress, but only after I got her to let go of my hand.

When Kim and I got out of the shower after some hot and steamy love making under the hot water, I was back, feeling like myself again.

I thought back to the conversation me, Rasul and Pretty E had when we were released from Gander Hill, and I really started understanding the conversation as I looked around my dinning room table at the smiling faces of my wife and kids. The feeling I was feeling right now as I spent time with my family was that there wasn't enough money in the world that could take its place. *You know what I might do? I might call it quits too,* I thought to myself.

But then I remembered all the work we had left on Vandever Avenue. "Man, fuck dat! I ain't never scared," I told myself, and then my phone rang. It was Mark, my Young Gunner.

Chapter Seven

"...Do I really want my baby?
Brother, tell me what to do.
I know you got to get yo' hustle on,
But I pray.
I understand the game sometime,
But our love is strong, Mmm, Hmm.

(Chorus)

What you gone do when they come for you?
Work ain't honest, but it pays the bills..."

"Other Side of the Game"
By: Erika Badu

I turned the volume up in my new S-Type Jaguar, and sang along with my favorite Erika Badu CD, "Baduism" as I drove away from Dog's house.

I really hoped that they understood that I was dead serious when I said that I'm done with the game. I didn't give a fuck about the fact that there is still work at the warehouse and the house on Vandever Avenue. I don't want anything to do with that shit; I don't even want any money from off that shit. It's time to fall back, invest some more of the money in some other shit like stocks and bonds, I.R.A. accounts, and mutual funds. I have to let some of my money grow in other ways besides the way it's growing now. I'm tired of having to keep looking over my shoulder while moving these drugs. I got to watch out for the police, the Feds, and these grimy niggaz out there, because I'm not untouchable. The same way I done banged niggaz up, duct taped them and robbed them for everything they had, that shit can happen to me too. This shit is dangerous, that's why the Mob doesn't fuck with the drug shit.

I used to ask Frankie all the time why he never dealt in the drug game like that, especially after seeing how much money we made and how fast we made it. But he never really had concrete answers. He would just say, "Because it's just something the five Families never indulged in," and I would just leave it at that. But I knew better than that shit. It just took me some time to figure out why, and eventually I came up with this conclusion:

Drugs were hot. Not hot like cool, but hot like bad. The police and all the powers that be in the United States of America had a system going on that was monopolizing, recycling, and changing up all the money in the economic system, while sending people to jail at the same time. The drug game was a dirty game. For every ten tons of illegal narcotics confiscated by U.S. Customs, the FBI, the Bay Authorities, and other government agencies, the United States already let one hundred tons onto its soil.

It took me a long time to figure out what the deal was with this drug shit, but I'm telling you, it's better to have found out now than to not have found out at all.

I also found out that on some real shit, drugs were really targeted at the Black communities anyway. Now all of the sudden, there's an urgency to so call stop the drug trade and fight a war on drugs, because the government's plan to destroy the Black communities backfired. They were now trying to save their own asses, because drug addiction hit their own communities. From as high up in the political seats as governor, down to the local paperboys, no one was exempt from the power of addiction. There was even a man who ran this entire country that openly testified against himself, stating that, "I smoked marijuana in college, but I never inhaled." Yeah, right!

Now drugs are becoming socially acceptable. The government even passed laws to prescribe marijuana to people for use as a medication, but they'd give a Black man a year in jail for two or three bags. Then on the cocaine part of this whole conspiracy, it's even worse.

Back in the early 1920's through the 1950's, cocaine was a drug for the elite. Only the most prominent people in society were able to get it. They used it when they hosted huge dinner parties, and they even made a soft drink out of it called "Coke Cola." Check the root word on the can; "Coke". I suggest you take a good look at this shit. I know this because I studied this shit. It's documented in U.S. history. I guess shit got out of control and people started understanding that you could get addicted to this shit, so they took it out of their recipe, and only the ones who wanted it could now buy it.

Over the years it elevated, and in the 1980's "crack" cocaine came along, burying us under the jails for that shit ever since. We get caught with two or three grams of that shit and get 5 to 10 years on a second offense, a year or two on the first, while the white boys get probation. See, I've done the math on this whole shit. I understand the consequences of the matter, and I understand that you need a stopping point, so I'm stopping. I got in, and now it's time for me to get out, because I've accomplished all that you can accomplish in this game without getting caught up.

I pulled my Jaguar into the three car garage and parked next to my wife's Range Rover, the one she insisted I buy her as a wedding gift, and my S.E. 600 Benz. Her Cadillac and Jaquaan's truck were in the driveway, so I knew they were home, and I was glad to be finally getting home myself, because my day had been long as hell.

I had been running around all morning long trying to make sure everything was in place at the banks and everywhere else in case they did get a bail, because I needed to get my boys out of there. I knew how it felt to be confined to a cage, a cell, a tier, or anything else, and I wouldn't wish that on my worst enemy, so you know I had to get my peoples out.

I walked through the front door of my new house, and every time I did, I'd see a different part of its beauty. Today, it was the waxed oak wood floors that you could see your face in, and the cathedral-like ceilings.

My wife was into her television and talking on the phone. I knew it was Tammy she was talking to, because I heard her talking about our vacation and how much they needed to go down there together one day for a weekend or something.

"Girl, let me call you back, hear? My husband just walked in, oka-a-a-ay?" she said into the phone, and laughed at her humorous response.

"Hey, baby!" I said. "What chu cookin'?"

"I'm already done cooking. I made some turkey wings, macaroni and cheese, and some cabbage. Why? You want me to make a plate for you right quick?"

"You can if you feel like it," I said.

"Why wouldn't I feel like it, baby?" she asked me, but I didn't answer. I figured I would take advantage of her mood while it was good, because by her being pregnant, it was sure to switch up sooner or later.

"Where you been at all day?" she asked me again as she brought me my food.

"Trying to post Dog and Pretty's bail."

"I thought they didn't have one."

"I told you yesterday when we was in Orlando that Lucy was coming back to defend them. So last night before we came home, she went to the Court Commissioner and was able to get them a new bail hearing."

"So, did they get one?"

"Yes, and I paid it. They'll be out in the morning." I lied for Pretty E, because I knew he was with Lucy. If Tammy found out he was home, she would have demanded that he get up to her house the moment he got out.

Over dinner, my wife and I had one of the deepest conversations we'd ever had since we've been together. We talked about life and the years ahead. We talked about the baby that was due in the next two months. We talked about Jaquaan and what college we were sending him to, and finally, we talked about me.

Tameeka's words over dinner were so strong to me that they cleared up any of the doubts I had left in the back of my mind, and assured me that I was making the right decision.

However, I still was thinking about my boys. We had been together our whole lives, but Tameeka made me realize that at a point in your life, you had to make a separation and live for yourself. I see clearly what she meant, because I have elevated mentally, matured faster, and educated myself to a point where we weren't on the same level in life anymore. Our lives were going in different directions. I was ready to fall back, and they were still knee-deep in the game.

"Baby," Tameeka said to me as I stuffed my face. "I know that Pretty E and Dog are your boys, just like Tammy is my girl. But baby, I've fallen back from her. When was the last time you saw us together? You haven't. I fell back from her because I'm a married woman, and she respects that, so she fell back too. I'm not saying you have to stop messing with Pretty E and Dog, I'm saying to you, just fall back for a minute. Enjoy me, enjoy me being your friend, your partner, your wife. Enjoy Jaquaan being your son. Baby, we're your family. We need you. We need you here with us."

"Right now, there is a lot of shit going on in their lives, and yours, even though you didn't get arrested with them. Check this out, baby. If you hang with nine broke friends, what's going to happen to you? You're right, you're bound to be the tenth one, so now let's flip it and bounce it. If the police think that your boys are selling drugs, what do you think they're going to think about you? Exactly! They're going to assume you're doing it too, and I don't need you getting jammed up. I need you here with me, for me and the baby. I would die if some 'em happened to you!" she finished, teary eyed.

"Ain't nothing going to happen to me, baby. I swear," I said to her, and reached across the table to grab her hand.

When I grabbed Tameeka's hand across the table, she clutched mine tightly and the feeling sent a chill up my spine. It was as if she had just transferred everything she was feeling over to me through her touch, and for the first time in my life, I felt the power of love and being loved by someone. Tameeka was my queen, and I was elated that she chose me to be her king, and as for my life right now, I couldn't see myself living a day without her.

I still remember the first time I saw her up Philly at that old nightclub, A Brave New World. Her dark milk chocolate complexion and gray eyes had me mesmerized to the point where I just stared at her.

"What chu starring at me for?" she asked me, but I was speechless.

I'm telling y'all, there are only three words that can describe my wife, and they are "drop dead gorgeous," and I'm wide open. My wife is the shit! She had me the first night we spent together at her house in Mount Erie. She had style, class, and attitude, and her house complimented her to a tee.

Her attitude though, was what stuck out to me the most. From the door, she staked her claim to the girls at the club by rudely telling them to step off and kick rocks. Then, she took charge of me by saying, "Come on, I'm ready to go home."

She had a lot of nerve to come off to me like that, not even knowing me like that. That's what really showed me her personality and take-charge mentality, because she saw what she wanted and went after it. I couldn't do nuffin' but comply with her. What was I going to say? "No, I ain't coming?" She even had the nerve to tell me to take off my shoes when I walked into her house. I'm telling you y'all, the girl had me from the gate. Then, she was almost ten years my senior, so she already knew how to treat a man from prior experience, but for me, it was all brand new.

I stood up from the table and walked over to the sink, carrying my plate to wash it, and before I could start, here comes my wife.

"Baby, go lay down. You've been up all morning long. I know you're tired. I got the dishes," she said, trying to take the plate from me.

"Nah, baby, I got this. Why don't you go lay down. You need to be off of your feet anyway, carrying all that weight around," I said, thinking about just how important my wife was to me. Here she was, knocked up and only two months away form her due date, and still trying to cater to me.

"You sure?"

"Yes, I'm sure. Now give me a kiss and go upstairs," I said, and gave her a wet, sloppy kiss in the mouth.

"Mmm! Damn, baby! You make me want to do what we do, kissing me like that!" she whined, and it sounded good to me.

"I know, huh?"

"Yep!"

"Well, come on then!"

"Last one upstairs is a rotten egg!" she said, and took off.

I laughed my ass off as I watched her wobble off, trying to run upstairs. You know I was the rotten egg, right?

Chapter Eight

After a week of lying up with Pretty E and studying the law books she had brought with her, she was ready for trial. Although it was only October, two months away from the appointed court date, she wanted to go now. She had come to the conclusion that a speedy trial would be the best defense for her and her clients, because that way it put a rush on the prosecution. They would have to prove their case, while all she had to do was prove their evidence wrong.

Lucy got in her car and left her new residence at Fox Run Apartments and Townhouses, and headed towards the city. She stopped at Dunkin Doughnuts and ordered two Boston cream doughnuts and a half pint of whole milk, then grabbed a newspaper. She took a seat at a table near a window and looked out over the busy Route 13 and Dupont Highway, and enjoyed her moment.

The doughnuts and her reading the paper had taken her mind off of the fact that Pretty E didn't come home last night for the second time this week. He had stayed with Tammy, and Lucy knew that because he didn't answer his phone all last night. The only time he did that was when he was with her, but she was getting used to it. He explained to her on more than one occasion that Tammy was a part of his life, and hers too if she wanted to be with him. She didn't mind that, because she knew Tammy was there first. What bothered her was the fact that he loved her.

Lucy tried everything in the world to compete with her lover's other woman, but no matter how hard she tried, she felt inferior to Tammy. Tammy had been there for too long, and had done too much for her to win. From some of the stories Pretty E had told her, Tammy had even brought drugs into the U.S. from other countries before, a feat way higher than Lucy would even dream of doing. Tammy was cut from a different cloth than she was, but she was determined to gain the same amount of love that Tammy received from him, if not more. *Besides, I'm having his baby,* she thought, and that put a smile on her face.

Lucy finished up her doughnuts and her paper, and left the fast food chain feeling optimistic. There was plenty of hope and plenty of Pretty E to go around. "I'm not worrying about Tammy," she said to herself as she pulled out onto Route 13. "There just better not be any other bitches, 'cause I'll fuckin' go berserk!" she tried to convince herself with her best attitude.

Lucy pulled up to the courthouse and parked across the street. It was Friday morning, sentencing day for most, and the courthouse was packed. She walked through the main doors and sighed a sigh of frustration at the line of people before her, all waiting to go through the metal detectors. Lucy was relieved to see that everyone else in the line must be thinking like her, because they flowed right through, and she followed and headed upstairs to the judge's chamber. Her motive was to deliver the motion she filled out for a speedy trial to Judge Silverstone.

Lucy walked in and took a seat on the couch in front of the secretary's desk, and grabbed a *People* magazine from off of the little end table. She started reading an article on Michael Jackson's child molestation charges as she waited on Judge Silverstone to call her to his chambers.

It was to her advantage that she'd come so early to deliver the paperwork, because if she would have come later, he would have been in trial. There was nothing better, she learned, than to give the judge all motions by hand instead of by mail or through a secretary, because you knew exactly when he or she got the motion. Plus, you were able to give the judge your spin on why it was so important to you, and why they should consider your matter at hand.

Poor Michael Jackson! I wish they would just leave him alone!" she thought as she read the article, and unconsciously started humming his song, "Just leave me alone."

"Ms. Vault, Judge Silverstone will see you now."

Judge Silverstone was sitting behind his desk, reading the *Wall Street Journal* and sipping coffee when Lucy walked into his office. His chamber was decorated with old model planes and trains, and pictures of the old courthouse and judges before him hung on the walls. Lucy stepped into his office slow and steady, as if the carpet was made of eggshells. She wasn't taking any chances on making the already no nonsense, straight by the book judge upset at all, because she needed him to hear her out. Needed to make the judge see things through her eyes. She knew that if she could just get him to grant this motion for a speedy trial, that would advance her chances of winning from a long shot to a favorite.

"Hello, Ms. Vault! How are you doing?" he asked.

"Fine, and yourself?"

"Oh, I'm fine, thank you."

"I'm not imposing myself on you in anyway, am I?"

"No, you're fine. Would you mind having a seat?"

"No, I wouldn't."

"So, Ms. Vault, tell me, what brings you to my chambers today?"

"Well, Your Honor, I've come this morning to hand deliver a motion for a speedy trial. I've already delivered one to the prosecution."

"I know, I have a copy of it here on my desk. In fact, I was just sitting here going over it," he said, and held it up for her to see.

"Well, let me give you this one I have here, so we can keep it on the legal aspect of things."

"Okay, that would be a good thing to do. Now tell me, Ms. Vault, why should I grant you the right to a speedy trial?"

"I think you should grant the motion because, Your Honor, this is clearly a case of personalization between my clients and Detective Cohen. If you look over the arrest report, Your Honor, you'll see clearly that Detective Cohen acted prematurely. There was no investigation done, or report on my clients. There was no warrant for their arrests, and to top it all off, there were three conflicting stories from the officers who were there on the day of the arrest. Judge Silverstone, I'm asking for this speedy trial, because I know how the police can be."

"And what might you mean by that? Are you insinuating something to me?"

"Your Honor, all I'm saying is that for the past eight years, I've been a federal agent. I just resigned recently because I saw how the law enforcement agencies work. I know that if they want you bad enough, they'd go to any lengths to get you. I fear that now, Your Honor. I fear that Detective Cohen may go to any lengths to get a conviction on my clients."

"Are you sure about this?"

"Yes, I'm sure, Your Honor, and to show you just how much, I don't want a jury trial. I want a bench trial."

"Here's what I'll do, Ms. Vault. I'm going to consider this motion over the next couple of days. Then, when I decide, you'll receive my response in the mail, okay? Now, if you'll excuse me, I have a trial to get ready for."

"Thank you Your Honor!"

■■■■■■

Tammy reached back and grabbed a handful of covers when the cold air hit her bare butt. She turned with them in her hand and nearly took all of them with her, leaving Pretty E exposed to the early morning chill. He scooted up next to her from behind, still half asleep, and inched up under the covers as far as he could without taking the covers off of her again. As soon as he got up next to her good enough, she pushed her ass up against his private parts and he lay his arm across her body.

For the past five years it had been this way. Tammy and Pretty E, even through all of their bickering and beefing, were inseparable.

Tammy turned to face Pretty E because she could no longer sleep. She scooted her body up into his until they fit into each other's arms like puzzle pieces. Their bodies were close, their legs were intertwined, and she could tell that this was where she belonged because it felt right. She was whole.

Tammy stared into Pretty E's face as he slept, and thought about Tameeka and Rasul. They were the happiest couple she knew, and their story, well, that was something from out of a fairytale. Two project kids from different cities who met each other at the re-starts of their lives, only to fall head over heels in love with one another and become successfully rich. The thing about their story that touched Tammy the most was that it was her story too. Their story was the same story she dreamed for herself as a child, and seeing Tammy live it only proved to her that her dream could become a reality too.

She knew the day that she met Pretty E on South Street in Dr. Denim's, that she was going to give the young boy some pussy. Women always know that. He was medium height for a man, the way she liked them. He had a light brown skinned complexion with waves in his hair, and big juicy lips like LL's. He also had deep dimples in both his cheeks, but the jump-off was that he was from Delaware. Tammy knew that none of her girls from Philly, her hometown, knew him, so that made for her a good keep.

"Damn, baby! Wha's your name?" he asked as she remembered the day.

Tammy turned and looked in the direction that the voice had come from, and saw some young boy staring at her with a pair of jeans in his hand. *Damn he's sexy!* she thought. *But he's a baby,* she assumed, because of the little mustache and fuzz under his chin. She knew from that he was well under her twenty eight years, but it didn't change the fact that he was sharp as tack.

Tammy was about to turn around and brush him off and get back to her business, but quickly changed her mind when he licked his lips. *Mmm, mmm, mmm!* she thought as she pictured those lips kissing her all over her body. *I'll turn his young ass out!*

"Damn, baby!" he said again. "What, you just going to ignore me like dat? How you just going to shoot me down like that without at least giving me a shot? You might be passing up your future husband and not even knowing it. But guess what? You'll know it ten years from now when you stuck with a lame," he finished, and she couldn't do anything but smile.

"Baby, you are crazy, and savvy to, huh? My name is Tammy."

"Hey, Tammy, my name is 'Your Man'! Nah, just joking. My name is Eric, but my friends call me Pretty E."

"Why?"

"I don't' know," he answered, and Tammy smiled again. She was happy to know that he wasn't conceited, because she knew clearly why they called him Pretty E, and he did to.

"Oh, so you don't know, huh?" she asked him.

"Nope. Why *you* think they call me that?"

"Boy, you a mess!" she said, staring into his face.

When Tammy's brief flashback was finished, she got out of the bed and went downstairs to make Pretty E some breakfast, taking the memory along with her.

■■■■■■

"Damn, playboy! What chu going to do?" Pretty E asked himself when he felt Tammy got out of bed. He was tired of lying to her everyday, especially when he knew that was one of the things she hated most. She preached to him all of the time about being honest, and respecting their relationship. She knew that her man was a man, and that all men will be men, she just wanted him to respect her, and to be honest about shit, because nothing hurt more than to hear it in the streets instead of hearing from your man first hand.

Pretty E got up and walked into the bathroom to brush his teeth when he smelled the breakfast cooking. He stared in the mirror, trying to find enough courage to tell her about Lucy, and finally found it. He had prepared himself mentally, because he knew Tammy was going to snap, especially when she found out Lucy was a white girl. The baby though, was the straw that might break the camel's back, but it was the truth. They had been trying to get pregnant for years now, but never could. In fact, just last week Tammy started on fertility drugs to increase their chances of having a child, and here it is, that he had some other woman pregnant.

Pretty E was confused to the point where he almost decided not to be truthful and let it go on for a couple more days—at least until he could build his courage up some more, but he decided to go forth with it. He put on his pajamas and headed downstairs to Tammy to explain the truth to her over breakfast. *Fuck it!* he thought as he walked out the bedroom door. *If she leaves, I still got Lucy.*

■■■■■■

Tammy was standing in front of the stove cooking breakfast in a half-cut T-shirt, thong, and some bunny rabbit slippers when Pretty E walked up behind her. He grabbed her from behind and gave her a hug and looked into the frying pan.

"Gimme a piece of bacon, baby," he said, and Tammy took the fork and picked a piece up. She shook the excess grease from the strip of meat and held it out for him to take, and he pinched it off the fork.

"Damn, baby, this bacon is bangin'! What is it? Turkey or that soy bean shit?"

"It's turkey today, baby."

"Oh!"

"Why don't you sit down and be patient. The food will be done in a minute," Tammy said as he reached for another piece.

"'Cause I'm hungry now."

"You always hungry," she said, and continued to get the food together.

Pretty E wasn't hungry, he was nervous. He couldn't think of any other way to spark up a conversation than the way he did.

Tammy walked over to the table and set his plate down in front of him, and asked him what he wanted to drink. When she came back, she had his glass of orange juice and her plate, and sat across from him to eat.

"Wha's wrong with you?" she asked between chews.

"Look baby. It's some shit going on with me that you need to know, but I don't know how to tell you," he responded.

"Tell me what?"

"Never mind."

"What chu mean, never mind? You should've never brought it up then."

"I said I don't know how to tell you."

"What chu mean, you don't know how to tell me? Be honest. I've always told you that, just be honest with me."

"Yeah, but I fucked up, baby. I fucked up real bad."

"What chu do?" Tammy asked, almost sick to her stomach with all the thoughts that ran through her head.

"Do you remember Lucy, the Fed lady?"

"Yeah, why?"

"I-I-I," he stuttered. "It's a long story."

"I got all day."

Pretty E looked at Tammy when she said what she said, and almost couldn't tell her. Her face looked stern, but there was a look of worry on her face that said she really didn't want to know.

"I'm waiting," she said, and lay her fork down on the table and folded her arms.

"Alright, Tammy. I met the babe, Lucy one night when we was at Li'l Italy, a bar on the west side, the night Frankie got out of jail."

"And?"

"And one thing led to another, and... well..." he paused to see her reaction before continuing. "I..."

"You what, Eric? What da fuck did you do, Eric?" she snapped as tears welled up in her eyes.

"I fucked up."

"You fucked dat bitch, didn't you?" she shouted, and he nodded his head "yes".

"I can't believe your ass! A white bitch at that! A muthafuckin' white bitch! You know what? You's a sorry no good bastard!" she said, and threw her plate in his face. "And after all that shit I've done for your ass, you got a nerve to fuck a white bitch!"

"Baby, I'm sorry," he said, and she burst into tears.

"So that makes it better?"

"Nah, it doesn't make it better, but it does let you know that I'm admitting my wrong, and that I'm apologizing for it."

A muthafucking white girl! she said to herself, not even hearing his apology. "You know what, Eric? I'm not even going to trip. I'm jut going to ask you to leave. Leave! Just get out of my house. I can't believe you. You make me not even want to look at you. I am so hurt right now, Eric. You have cut me deeply, to the point where I really have nothing to say to you right now. I just want you to go."

"Baby, I—"

"Look, Eric, just leave," she said, cutting him off. "Get out of my face. I'm trying so hard right now not to snap and cut your stupid ass. It's pathetic. But you know what? I got your muthafucking ass!" she said, getting angrier with each word she spoke. "You going to pay for this shit though. Watch."

"What, chu threatening me or some 'em?"

"No, I'm not threatening you at all, because I would never stoop to your level. I got some 'em for you, though."

"What?"

"None of your business. I'm sure you'll figure it out. I ain't fuckin' with you no more. Let dat white bitch take care of your ass. Oh, and I'll take your clothes and shit over to Rasul and Tameeka's house. Now, can you please leave?" she finished, and Pretty E stood to leave.

He looked back over his shoulder at Tammy and turned to leave out the door, and she fell apart. Her fake, strong Black woman act went straight out the window, and was replaced with a woman who needed strength, a woman who needed a hug, a woman who was lost, and didn't know what to do, a woman who loved the man she just made walk out of her life.

Chapter Nine

Rasul's words weighed heavy on their ears over the past week and a half, but they still didn't change the fact. The fact was that they just weren't ready to give the game up yet. The money was too plentiful and easy to maintain for them to just up and leave it alone like Rasul did, leaving them puzzled about how he came to that decision so easily. "I guess we're ain't where he's at yet in life," they both agreed on more than one occasion.

Dog and Pretty E had been talking every day about how they had to do things different. They clashed on many of the ideas, but they eventually came to an agreement on one, so they decided to meet at the stash house to get the ball rolling.

Thirty-six forty-one Vandever Avenue, the stash house located in the dead center of the city, had to be moved. The reason, the investigating eye of the law had penetrated their comfort zone. The plan they came up with was to hurry up and move the rest of the bricks from out of the house and transfer them to the new spot, Michelle's Hair Styles, the beauty salon Pretty E brought for Michelle, his young jawn. He had already placed her on point and prepared her for the drop-off, in which she would then transfer the bricks down into the projects to Monk and Shay-Ball. The sooner they could make this happen, the sooner they could get the money rolling and put an end to the drought.

Their arrest two weeks ago had put a major dent in Wilmington's drug supply, so when the news hit that they were home, their phones began ringing off the hook. Dealers from everywhere were calling them, and it wasn't a secret why. They were calling because the price of cocaine had skyrocketed to unbelievable rates. An ounce of cocaine that Rasul, Dog, and Pretty E were letting go for six hundred, to six hundred and fifty, was now going for a stack to twelve hundred. That was going to change though, because Dog and Pretty E were back.

Dog circled the block thrice before he noticed Pretty E's car parked around the corner from the house. He did this every time he came to the stash house, because he wanted to know who he was in the company of. He wanted to know if the house was under surveillance of any kind, whether it was from the police or the stick-up kids, because they weren't exempt.

Dog parked his car behind another parked car with a flat tire, and then cursed himself for not doing this the day they got jammed up. Had he circled the block then, he more than likely would have seen the police waiting on them. He reached over the seat and grabbed the newspaper from off of the back seat to cover his head up. He placed it as best he could up on the top of his head and held it up there as he got out of the car into the rain. Dog high-stepped through the rain and over the mess of puddles that were accumulating on the sidewalks and in the streets before finally making it onto the porch of 3641 Vandever Avenue.

"Wha's up, nigga? Why you here so early? We wasn't supposed to meet here until three," Dog said, looking at the time on his watch.

"Man, me and Tammy just got finished arguing about some dumb shit," Pretty E answered.

"What?"

"I told her about Lucy."

"And you think that's dumb shit?"

"Damn right that's some dumb shit, especially since she knows how I feel about her."

"Nigga, I told you a long time ago about fuckin' with all those bitches. What is Michelle going to say when she finds out about Lucy?"

"Nothing, because Michelle knows her position."

"Okay, well that's one out of how many? See, you be doing it to yourself. Look at you, all caught up in your feelings and shit. You know what my Pop had always used to tell me, nigga?" Dog continued. "Don't be with the woman you love. Be with the woman that loves you, that way if she decides to leave your dumb ass, it won't hurt as bad. Feel me?"

"Damn, that shit was deep! You should've been told me some shit like that."

"You had me fooled, nigga. I thought you was a P.I.M.P. or some shit. Plus, sometimes you gotta find out some shit on your own." "I heard that. So, wha's up? You ready to do this?"

"Yeah, let's hurry up and get this shit over with," Dog said, heading out into the kitchen.

Pretty E grabbed his keys out of his pocket and opened the lock that ran through the cabinet handles, and Dog put the bricks in the duffel bag. He slung it over his shoulder and said," Damn, cousin! It's fucked up we gotta close down the Carter," as he gave the house a once over.

"I know, huh? This is where it all began," Pretty E said.

"Yeah, right here in these chairs," Dog said aloud, but not directing it in any way.

"Now all we gotta do is call the realtors and get this muthafucka on Section 8," Pretty E said as they headed for the door. "Then the Carter will still be making money, only this time eight-hundred a month," he continued, and they both smiled.

■■■■■■

Detective Cohen's beard was wild, full grown, and unkempt. The five o'clock shadow he used to sport was gone. His eyes were red and puffy from the bags that grew underneath them from a lack of sleep, and his lack of sleep set off an attitude towards everyone around him. Every little thing that could possibly irritate a person had irritated him, from way down to his wife not putting the toilet seat up after she used it, clear up to the long line at the WaWa's gas station this morning, had Cohen mad.

He couldn't believe that the judge granted bail to Pretty E and Dog, especially after all the allegations he and the prosecutor had presented to the court. So what if they caught the charges when they were juveniles? The fact was that they had committed the same types of acts before and had been convicted of them. Now all of a sudden they were caught red-handed with two kilos of cocaine and some automatic weapons. Cohen knew, as well as he knew the courthouse knew, that it didn't take a rocket scientist to figure out that Pretty E and Dog were known drug dealers.

Detective Cohen got up from his office desk and walked down to the Forensics Department to check on the ballistics from the guns. He kind of knew that the guns were probably already clean, but, *What the hell?* He thought, as he tried to help out in any way he could.

The prosecutor told him the day the bail was granted that this was going to be a highly profiled case, and that they needed to be flawless. The more Kevin Donavan talked about the case, the more Cohen felt the case was personal to him as well. He thought back on the day bail was granted, and remembered the conversation like they just had it yesterday...

"Hey, Donavan!" Cohen called out to him before he walked off in a different direction. "Can I ask you a question?"

"Shoot!" he responded.

"Seems to me that this case is a little personal to you. May I ask, are my intuitions right?"

"Just a little bit."

"May I ask why?"

"Yes, you may. Did you see the new attorney that the defendants hired?"

"Yes, I remember her."

"Oh! Then let's just say that I was planning on changing her last name to 'Donavan,' but she broke it off."

"Wow, are you serious? Damn, I'm sorry to hear that. I've had my run-in with her also."

"Really?"

"Yeah, she took over the homicide case I had in Colony North in which there were four men brutally assassinated. It was one of the bloodiest murder cases in the city's recent history. I had a suspect by the name of Hakeem Stewart, AKA Hit-Man, in custody and about to be charged with the crime, but she took over the entire case."

"What happened to the case?"

"There was none, because right after she took over, he committed suicide in a safe house."

"Are you serious?"

"Dead serious."

"Why was he taken to a safe house?"

"That's the part that still puzzles me to this day. I do know that he had some kind of ties with the Mob."

"The Mafia?"

"Yes, that's why I know that Pretty E and Dog are involved in some kind of way too, because they were a team. The leader of them though, is a guy name Rasul. I haven't seen him lately."

"Where is he?"

"I don't know. I haven't seen him since the day I watched him board a plane, and I arrested Dog and Pretty E."

"So, what do you think happened to him?"

"Nothing. I think he's smart," Cohen finished as they walked their separate ways...

Cohen left the Forensics Department empty-handed, just as he imagined he would. The guns were clean; so clean that their fingerprints weren't even on them.

He didn't get discouraged though. He just looked to the sky and talked to his partner again. "Hey, ol' buddy! How's heaven treating you?" he asked his partner, Detective Armstrong, as if he was still alive and well.

"I bet it sure beats this hell, doesn't it? Anyways, I'm just talking to you now because I wanted to let you know that even thought it's been over two years since you been gone, I'm still going strong. I won't let your murder go unsolved as long as there's breath in my body, you hear?"

"Yeah, I hear you," Detective Reed answered when he saw Cohen talking to himself.

"Oh shit!" Cohen jumped, startled by the voice. "How long have you been standing there?"

"Long enough for me to know how much you miss your partner, Armstrong."

"Yeah, I miss him dearly. He was my teacher."

Chapter Ten

The Liacoros Center in North Philadelphia Temple University Sports Complex, was where the Philadelphia Public League High School Basketball Championship was being held. Since it was a sporting event, Rasul and Tameeka decided to drive their sports utility vehicle to the affair. Franklin Learning Center, Jaquaan's high school, was playing Bartrum High School for the title. Rasul drove down Broad Street towards the complex through heavy traffic, and knew that it was because of the game.

This was Jaquaan's senior year, his last high school basketball game, so he had to put on a show. At six foot seven inches tall, he sprouted up in the air nearly five inches over the summer, so he was a good college hopeful. Jaquaan's game was nice where it was right now, because it was just raw natural talent. But with some polish over the summer break, he could easily become a standout next year in college. Rasul knew that, so he contacted a few people he knew and got him a spot at a camp in Texas run by Tim Duncan. The Camp of Big Fundamentals was the name, and that's just what Jaquaan needed some fundamentals. A little more floor vision and some unselfish play and his game could become Dwayne Wade-like, because it already had glimmers of it. It just had to come out.

Rasul pulled up to the front of the sports complex and let Tameeka out because he didn't want to make her walk. She had been complaining about her feet and ankles already, so making her walk would surely trigger off one of her mood swings. "Baby, keep your phone on so I can call you when I get back from parking the truck," he said, and pulled away from the curb.

Rasul began to smile for no apparent reason at all. He just was feeling good about life today, feeling good about being married. He felt good about having a family, felt good about being out of jail, and felt good about being free from the game. Family life was the key to his happiness, and he was finally finding that out more and more every day.

Tameeka was his lifeline, his support system, his best friend, and his other half. There was no way his life could go on without her, and he knew it. She was the reason for his success. She was his balance, his backbone and his rationale. Tameeka made more than half of his major decisions. Without her, there was no him.

Rasul parked the truck.

■■■■■■

Tameeka walked into the Liacoros Center and was surprised to see all the people who came out to see the game. By the look of the crowd, you would have thought that Allen Iverson or somebody was playing tonight, instead of two high school teams. The entire ground level and first level of the sports complex was completely full.

Damn! None of our high school games were packed like this! She thought back to her high school days. The funny thing about it though, was that 17 years ago, when she was still in school, it felt like yesterday. *Damn, I was only sixteen or seventeen back in my days of Strawberry Mansion High School,* she remembered in bewilderment.

Tameeka looked around the gymnasium for her sister, Erica and her girlfriends, and spotted them behind Franklin

Learning Center's bench. They each were showing their team support by wearing blue sweatshirts with the letters F.L.C. in white trimmed in silver across the front as they waited for the game to begin. She was almost over to where they were seated when she heard the ever so familiar voice call her name.

"Hershey!"

Tameeka stopped dead in her tracks and looked up into the seats. "Where's he at?" she asked herself, trying to find him.

"Hershey!" she heard him call again, but she still couldn't find him through all the people. It was like trying to find a needle in the haystack.

"Fuck it!" she said. "If he wants me, he sees me, so he'll come to me," and continued to her seat. Then out of nowhere, he popped up.

Jahlil still looked the same way he did now as he did in high school. He and Tameeka both looked more like they were in their twenties rather than their thirties, and they were glad to see each other. They hadn't seen each other in months until now, and he was surprised at how big she had gotten.

"Hey, Hershey, how you doing?" Jahlil asked.

"Don't call me Hershey, boy! I ain't your candy bar no more," she laughed.

"You always going to be my Hershey chocolate bar. Nobody, not even my wife can change that. You will always be my friend, and I'm fond of our memories together. I remember them every time I look at our son."

"It's nice to know that our memories are good ones. I tend to reminisce at times myself. How's your wife doing?" Tameeka asked the spitting image of her son.

"She's fine. She's right there with our daughters. The girls would have died if they didn't get a chance to see their brother play," Jahlil said, and Tameeka's phone went off. After she let Rasul know where she was, she got back to the conversation with Jahlil. "Now, where were we at?"

"We were at the girls."

"Oh, that's right. Where are they at again?" Tameeka asked, and he pointed to them.

"There they are," he said.

Tameeka looked up at them, and when they made eye contact, she waved at his wife, Sabiyah, dressed in *Hijab*. *Hijab* was the garb that Muslim women wore, and the daughters were dressed in them too. All three of them looked nice in the garments that covered their bodies and their faces, and Jahlil looked good in his garment too. He wore a *Thobe*, something similar to the ones his wife and kids were wearing, except it was made for men. His beard was long, full and groomed to perfection, and he smelled so good that Tameeka found herself lusting over him for a split second.

Girl, get a grip! she reminded herself as she realized just how weak the flesh can be. Here she was, happily married, and the devil still made a way to bring temptation into her life. She knew right then and there that she needed a higher power in her life, and she was sure going to share it with her husband later on tonight when she got home.

Then the phrase, "A family that prays together, stays together," came to her mind, and for the first time in her life, she saw how that worked. God was the only one who could keep temptation away.

Rasul walked over to where he saw his wife standing, and walked up to stand at her side. The Muslim brother she was standing with was tall and had to look down on him when he approached. He gave the brother the once-over, but didn't recognize him from anywhere. He did, however, remind him of somebody he knew, but he just couldn't put a finger on it. Maybe he remembered him from the Fed joint or something, but asking the brother something like that would be more than inappropriate.

"Hey, baby, wha's up?" Rasul asked Tameeka as he walked up to her side and gave her a kiss on the cheek.

"Oh, hey, baby! Let me introduce you to someone," she said, and began. "Rasul, this is Jahlil, Jaquaan's father. Jahlil, this is my husband, Rasul."

And right then, Rasul knew where he knew him from. He looked just like Jaquaan. "As-Salaam-Alaikum! It's nice to meet you. Jaquaan has told me a lot about you. I've been looking forward to meeting you," he said, and the two shook hands.

"I've been looking forward to meeting you too."

"Baby, look. My feet hurt. I need to go sit down somewhere. Why don't y'all get to know each other better," Tameeka intervened, and then walked off.

"Go ahead, we alright," Rasul said, and watched her walk away.

"Now, as I was saying," Jahlil spoke. "My son speaks highly of you. I'm glad that Tameeka chose you as her husband, good brother, and not some knucklehead. It seems as if you got your head on straight. I've done my homework on you, and I haven't received anything but praises. That's not to say that I was spying on you or anything like that. It was just my fatherly instincts kicking in, and the concern for my child.

"That's understandable. I've done my homework on you too. I'm just hoping that my career ends as successfully as yours did, you know?" Rasul said.

"God willing. You just have to know when to hold them, and when to fold them."

"I heard dat!" Rasul replied.

Rasul had done the research on Jahlil a long time ago, when he first started messing with Tameeka. What he found out was that Jahlil was an ex kingpin who had retired from the game after a long stretch in Graddaford State Penitentiary. He owned two restaurants, a sneaker store on South Street that was doing pretty good next to Foot Locker, and a barber shop in North Philly. He didn't have as much money as Rasul did, but he was doing well for himself and his family. That's what Rasul meant when he said he hoped his career ended like his did. He wanted to get out and be comfortable with just being able to support his family, and from the looks of things, he was on the right track.

"What do you think tonight's outcome is going to be?" Jahlil asked.

"I don't' know. I've never seen Bartrum play. I do know that Jaquaan got a game though."

"Yeah, he's all right. He just needs some more work."

"I feel you. I mean, the raw natural ability is there, it just needs to be fine-tuned. Oh, and while I'm thinking about it, look. I called my mans and them down Forth Worth, Texas, and they said there's a camp called Camp Big Fundamentals run by Tim Duncan. I got him in there. What do you think?"

"That's all good, but how much does it cost? Look, brother. I'm not going to let you keep footing the bill and outdoing me," Jahlil smiled. "You already brought the boy a truck."

"Nah, nah, man. It ain't nothing like that," Rasul smiled, catching the joke. "I just know how it is when you fall back and ain't making no noise anymore."

"Well, at least let me pay half."

"Alright, you got that," Rasul said, and the two shook hands and went to their seats.

"You alright?" Tameeka asked Rasul when he sat down next to her.

"Yeah, I'm good," Rasul said, and the buzzer sounded for the game to begin.

■■■■■■

The game ended differently than anyone in the Liacoros Center expected. The Franklin Learning Center team was clearly outclassed in the second half by a Bartrum team that was supposed to lose, and lose big. The final score was 77 to 60, a devastating loss to the Franklin team that was full of seniors and last year's defending champions.

Jaquaan was torn to pieces as he sat on the bench along with the rest of the starters that the coach took out with a minute left so they could receive their standing ovation for four years of excitement and two championships.

Rasul walked down to the court when the buzzer sounded, and held Jaquaan in his arms as he cried. "Come on, man. It's only a game. Tighten up. The girls are looking at you and shit. You don't want them to see you crying, do you?" he chuckled, bringing Jaquaan to a smile. "Plus, you had a real good game. Twenty-two points, thirteen rebounds, and four assists. The scouts had to love that," Rasul said to him as Jahlil came down to meet with them.

"Wha's up, Dad? As-Salaam-Alaikum!"

"Wa-Laikum Salaam! You had a real good game. I'm proud of you."

"Thanks," he replied, and hugged his little sisters.

"Are you coming to the house before you leave Philly?"

"Why, wha's up?"

"Because Sabiyah cooked your favorite. Rasul, you and Tameeka are more then welcome to come too."

"I'm going to have to pass this time. I have something to do today and tonight."

"Okay, maybe we'll do it some other time."

"Yeah, maybe. Or you can come down to our house. Either way, we'll hook up on that."

"Okay, that's a bet."

"Dad, what did she make?"

"Oooh, Dad! Can we tell him?" India and Asia, Jaquaan's two little sisters, said in unison.

"Yeah, go ahead."

"She made turkey chops, broccoli, macaroni and cheese, and fried brown rice," India said.

"And for dessert, she made carrot cake with thick icing," Asia added.

"Mmmm! After all that ballin' I just did, I'm hungry as a mutha—" Jaquaan said, catching himself.

"I am too," Jahlil said. "Oh, and try to get there before six-thirty because that's when *Mahgrib* prayer comes in. Maybe we can make it together."

"Okay, Dad, I'll try," Jaquaan said, and his dad and sisters walked off.

"You alright now?" Rasul asked Jaquaan.

"Yeah, I'm cool."

"That's wha's up! Oh, I knew I had some 'em to tell you."

"What?"

"I got you in a camp. A top notch camp too."

"Where at?" Jaquaan asked.

"In Texas."

"Say word?"

"Word," he replied. "It's Tim Duncan's camp."

"Thanks, Rasul! Man!"

"You're welcome."

"Rasul, I love you!" he said, and ran off with his team to the lockers.

"I love you too!" Rasul yelled, then thought, *Let me go get this car before my wife starts bitchin',* and headed out of the Liacoros Center.

Chapter Eleven

The infamous Li'l Italy Bar and Lounge located on Wilmington's Hilltop section of the city, was a known hangout for mobsters and wise guys, but it didn't stop Frankie from calling a meeting there. He had a policy that had become law ever since he became the boss of all bosses, so why change it. *What better way to conduct business than right out in the open,* he thought as he sat at a table in the back of the lounge, surrounded by the Capelli Family.

He called this meeting with the Family because of the upcoming trial for Pretty E and Dog. He wanted to get everyone in the Family on the same page so it didn't look like he was holding anything away from them. He was aware of Lucy's return before she even got back, because Rasul had told him about it. His initial thought was to 'hit' her the moment she touched ground in Wilmington, but Rasul persuaded him out of that. He sold a hell of a story to Frankie to convince him to let her live, but he promised him that the day the trial was over, it was his job to kill Lucy.

Frankie took a long sip of Tuaco, a very expensive Italian liquor, and looked out at his Family. They looked back into the boss's eyes, but he didn't say anything. He was too busy trying to assess the information he was ready to dispense to the Family in a way they could at least understand it before he blurted out some shit that would have had them questioning his decisions.

I gotta tell them some 'em, he thought, because he knew by just the way the bail hearing turned out that this was going to be a huge trial and media circus. He knew that if the Family got the news anywhere else other than the boss, they would have said he was slipping or losing touch with the streets. That wouldn't have gone well at all, because that's what Frankie prided himself on. He was selected as the boss because of that.

He stalled for a little more time as thoughts of the headlines to come flashed like pictures through his mind:

*EX-FEDERAL AGENT BACK
TO DEFEND KINGPINS!*

*EX-FEDERAL AGENT AND KINGPIN
ARE LOVERS!*

*EX-FEDERAL AGENT PAYED OFF
BY BOSS OF BOSSES!*

*BOSS OF BOSSES GUNNED DOWN IN
COLD BLOOD BY OWN FAMILY!*

That last thought was what scared him the most, because he knew it to be true. The same people who were sitting right here at the round table with him would be the same ones to put a bullet in the back of his ear before he dishonored *La Cosa Nostra*.

Frankie told them everything, from the time he knew about Lucy's return to the moment he knew about her role as their lawyer, and it didn't seem to matter. They didn't mind that Lucy was back to defend their extended family of Dog, Pretty E and Rasul, even though he wasn't on trial. They didn't care that the trial would probably be plastered all over the newspapers and television sets. The only thing they cared about was that she didn't leave again… alive anyway. They wanted Lucy dead, and that's all. Her actions from the past were not forgotten for one moment, because for the next seventeen years, Lenny (Fat Boy) Ionni was jammed up in the "can" for some bullshit. Lucy's indictment was enough to get a conviction and sentence, now she would repay the Family with her life.

"Who's going to hit her?" Joey (The Fox) Vito asked, rubbing his hands together.

"Yeah, who's going to hit her?" Ricky Stango asked, as he smiled and turned towards his brother.

"Rasul is," Frankie replied. "Since he was the one who got her back."

"Lucky him," Nicky said. "'Cause I want to ring her neck myself."

"We all do, we all do," Frankie said, relieved that everything went smoothly.

"*Scusa!*" he said, which meant "excuse me" in his native Italian tongue, and got up to leave the table. He walked to the back of the lounge and entered into the room marked "Members Only," the same room he met with Rasul, Dog, Pretty E, and Hit-Man the day he was released from prison, and walked over to the desk where he conducted his business. He took a seat in the old swivel chair with the orange filling busting from its torn fabric, and reached into its drawer. He grabbed the prescription bottle given to him by his doctor, and shook one of the tiny pills into his hand. His illness was much more than the prostate cancer he told his Family and Rasul about. He had a bad heart, and as he looked at the small pill no larger than a cookie crumb, he began to pray:

"Please, God," he began. "Please grant me some more life." But the reality remained the same. Frankie was growing older by the day. He grabbed the half-full bottle of cranberry juice, popped the pill in his mouth and tilted his head back as the nitroglycerin tablet slid down his throat. It was the only thing that could jumpstart his heart when it stopped or felt like it would, and just knowing that made him worried.

Chapter Twelve

The courtroom was occupied by more than twice the amount of people who were there to attend the bail hearing. Today, everyone from the families of Dog and Pretty E, to the ex-partners of Lucy who were there to support them, and a crowd full of media writers, news reporters, and spectators, all there to feed their desires for the need of sensationalism. These were the people with no excitement in their own lives. These were the people who went about the town spreading all types of gossip and nonsense about any and everybody who was in a better position in life than they were in. The crazy part was that they did these things just to have something to say.

Lucy stepped into the parade of people, looking dapper as usual with her hair pulled up into a bun. The Chanel pants set she wore fitted loosely but revealingly, as she stood tall in her Salvatore Faragomo boots. A few flashbulbs went off as the media snapped shots of her, but that was quickly put to a halt by a bailiff who made it clear that there would be no more pictures taken inside the courtroom.

Lucy made her way through the media circus and down to the defense table, and looked over at Donavan, who was doing some kind of paperwork shuffle, and flashed a confident smile. Today was her day; the day that she yearned for, studied for, and stayed up all hours of the night for trying to find loopholes in any way she could. She found them too, and she was sure that the judge would see them also. There was no way in the world he could find them guilty. She knew it deep down in her heart.

■■■■■■

Prosecutor Donavan smiled back at Lucy, but his smile was more devilish than confident, more sinister than honest. He smiled like he had a trick up his sleeve, and he probably did, because he was known to play dirty. On more than one occasion he had printed up fake documents with arresting officers to tighten up loopholes in cases he was sure to lose. As a result, he became the leading prosecutor in the State, and built a reputation so large that he was sure to be a shoe-in for governor if he ran for the office.

Donavan took a sip of his water, glared over at Lucy and shook his head. *The bitch gotta be crazy!* he thought to himself. *How can she leave me or not give me the time of day, and then get knocked up by some thug?* He paused as he looked at her stomach and let his thoughts sink in. *I'll teach her ass a thing or two today though, especially when the judge finds these two motherfuckers guilty on all charges,* he finished, as his true feelings surfaced; the ones he thought he had buried years ago.

■■■■■■

Pretty E and Dog walked into the courtroom about five minutes after Lucy and ten minutes before the trial was supposed to start. The media circus had just calmed down and settled in for the trial to begin when they appeared, only to get them aroused again. The commotion, however, wasn't directed towards them, it was directed towards their company, the Boss of all Bosses, Mr. Frankie Maraachi.

Frankie stepped into the courtroom behind Dog and Pretty E with Joey (The Fox) Vito at his side, and took a seat behind the defense. Dressed in a funeral parlor black Armani suit and trench coat with a white scarf dangling endlessly, he was the center of attention. His huge hands were decorated at the pinkies by two enormous size diamond stones that flickered like the sun dancing on a lake. His presence alone, along with his under boss, was so overpowering that it literally sucked all the air out of the courtroom.

Prosecutor Donavan looked at the two intimidating forces in the courtroom, and for no apparent reason, fear gripped him for the first time in his illustrious career as a prosecutor. He looked over at Frankie, who was talking to the guy next to him, who he later found out from Detective Cohen to be Rasul.

The short guy, however, was the one who captured his attention. He was sneaky, almost too sneaky. Sneaky to the point were Donavan thought he was up to no good. He did a couple more paperwork shuffles hoping to escape the stare of the short guy with the stone-faced stare, but it didn't work. He could still feel the short guy's eyes stuck to his body. He lifted his head to face his intimidator hoping the stare-down would stop, but the moment he made eye contact with Joey (The Fox) Vito, his fears became confirmed.

Joey lifted an imaginary pistol and squeezed his trigger finger two times at Donavan, and Donavan almost choked. He looked to the bailiff to see if he saw what just took place, but he didn't. He then looked to the cop, but he didn't see it either.

Donavan was all alone in a crowded courtroom full of people, all by himself. There was no way in the world that he was going to forward with trial the way he planned it after a gesture like that. His life was more important to him than just putting two thugs behind bars or getting some job in office as governor. His life was priceless, and he wasn't going to sell himself out, not today or any day to come. He was willing to take this loss on the chin. *I still may be able to win a seat in office,* he thought, and took his seat at the prosecution table.

■■■■■■

Lucy was getting her opening statements together when she heard the buzz through the courtroom. The light tapping of fingers on the computer keyboards, the soft sounds of rattling paper, and the few whispers in the courtroom were overshadowed by murmurs of the media. She turned in the direction of the voices, and there coming down the isle was her lover, his friend, and Frankie Maraachi. Behind them were Joey Vito and Rasul. The initial shock of seeing her used to be worst enemy and the person she dedicated two years of her life to towards trying to put behind bars, gave her mixed feelings. The one side of her felt bad, because everything she had worked so hard for fell apart, but the other side of her felt good, because everything went well for him because he was still a free man. That's where she had developed a soft spot for saving the "bad guy".

"Hey, baby!" she said in a hushed tone as Pretty E and Dog took their seats at the defense table.

"Hey, wha's up? You ready to do this shit?"

"Yeah, I'm ready. There's no way we won't be cleared from all charges today," she said confidently.

"I heard that!" Dog said.

"Why is Frankie here?" Lucy asked Pretty E, and instantly, everything she had done in the past came back to haunt her. Her big mouth had reminded Pretty E of everything she had made him forget over the past two months, and as she stared into his face, his eyes cut right through her.

"Why?" he asked sharply, but she wisely responded, "Never mind," and was saved by the bailiff.

"All rise! The Honorable Judge Silverstone is now presiding," and the entire courtroom stood to its feet.

Since this was a bench trial, the jury box was empty, but every other seat in the courtroom was occupied.

The extra security that was present was because of the heavily covered incident that went on in downtown Atlanta. A man overpowered a female guard, took her gun and shot and killed the judge, a federal agent, and another person before fleeing the courthouse, and Delaware wasn't taking the chance on a copy-cat.

Judge Silverstone looked out into his courtroom, and saw which was by far the biggest trial he had ever seen or had to preside over. He set his huge stainless steel thermos up on his bench, sat in his leather swivel chair, and grabbed his gravel. "You may be seated," he said into the small microphone on the bench, and like dominos, they all went down. "Prosecution, you may state your case."

"Your Honor," Donavan began. "Today I will prove without a reasonable doubt that the defendants, Michael Lollie and Eric Benson, are known drug dealers and kingpins. I will prove to you, Your Honor, that the day the Wilmington Police Department's Vice Squad stopped them and made the arrest, they were found with two kilos—two thousand grams—of powdered cocaine, and two semiautomatic weapons. I will prove to you that the defendants have no trail of paperwork leading back to the numerous businesses they own, or their other assets. Your Honor, no one in the world has been able to attain so much from nothing. I mean, these two never even had a job. In fact, the only way to obtain the amount of assets they have is to inherit it, invent something, or hit the Power Ball. Only it came in balls of cocaine."

"Thank you, Mr. Prosecutor. Are you finished?" Judge Silverstone asked.

"Yes, I am."

"Defense, you may state your case."

"Good morning, Your Honor," Lucy spoke. "Your Honor, I'm here today to defend two innocent victims accused of being drug kingpins. I will prove to you today that the defendants, Mr. Michael Lollie and Mr. Eric Benson, are the victims of an ongoing plot to be framed by an officer of the law. Detective Cohen, leader in the department of vice officers, lost a partner several years ago, and he has been harassing my clients ever since. I will prove to Your Honor today that this is a clear case of nonsense and a perfectly planned frame. All the evidence in this case has been fingerprinted and none of the prints match my clients."

"Your Honor, I asked for this bench trial myself, because I didn't need a jury to distort their thinking or try to win a case with a unanimous decision. All I need is you, Your Honor. I'm sure you'll make a conscious decision yourself. Thank you."

"Is that it, Ms. Vault? Are you finished your opening statements?"

"Yes, I am."

And the trial began.

Prosecutor Donavan started the trial off by displaying the evidence found during the stop. The two kilos and semi-automatic weapons that he put on the table made the spectators start up a small conversation amongst themselves, but the money that was found was what made the judge bang down his gavel and yell, "Order!" There were two large plastic Zip-lock bags full of cash totaling sixty-two thousand dollars.

"Where would they just get that amount of money from? Better yet, why would anybody in their right mind be driving into the Riverside Housing Projects with that type of money in their possession? Wouldn't a bank be a more appropriate stop?" Donavan said, making a strong statement, but not strong enough to the point where it would stick. He knew Lucy would be able to counter this claim, because they did have legitimate businesses. That was why he used it. He wanted to give her enough room and space to counter everything he said, because he didn't want to win. The death threat from the short guy was still fresh on his mind. He remembered the look in his eyes and the way he pointed the imaginary gun at him, and realized his life was still way more valuable than just winning some trial.

For the rest of his presentation of the case he had against Dog and Pretty E, Donavan stayed just above the surface. He never went deep into the core of the case, because he knew there was a chance she could lose. He did, however, make the case look interesting enough to where it looked like he fought the best fight of his life as he called detective after detective, until he reached Detective Cohen. After Cohen shared his account of what happened on the day of the arrest, he rested his case.

Lucy knew that the case Donavan was presenting was as weak as water. She didn't even have to present her best argument, but she was going to anyway. She wanted to make a statement. Any time Donavan presented something new or called a witness, she objected or cross-examined. It was clearly an all-out battle between prosecutor and lawyer in the courtroom, and the underdog was clearly winning. The knockout blow came when Detective Cohen hit the stand though, because she knew his history and the grudge he held for her clients.

"Detective Cohen, how long have you been a detective?" she cross-examined.

"About six years," he replied

"How long have you known my clients?"

"About three years."

"How do you know them?"

"From my old partner."

"Your old partner. Who?"

"Detective Armstrong."

"Where is this Detective Armstrong? Is he here today?"

"No, he isn't. He's deceased."

"Oh my! I'm sorry to hear that," she said as she dug into some paperwork. "Would this Detective Armstrong happen to be the same officer found dead at a robbery scene a few years ago?"

"Yes," Cohen answered, gritting his teeth.

"Oh, so this Detective Armstrong is the same officer whom the department labeled a 'crooked cop', and cleared all the open cases of robberies and homicides from their books and labeled him the culprit?"

"I object! Your Honor, what does this have to do with this case?" Donavan blurted out.

"Ms. Vault, you may proceed. Just get to the point."

"Thank you, Your Honor." She continued. "Detective Cohen, you believe my clients were there that night, don't you? You believe, in fact, that my clients are the ones who did that to your partner, don't you? Are you a crooked cop yourself, Mr. Cohen?"

"I object! Defense is antagonizing the witness!"

"Isn't it true that you planted the drugs and weapons on my clients to set them up as a revenge of your partner's death? Aren't you lying, Detective?" Lucy yelled, and Cohen fell apart.

"Listen here, you li'l bitch!" he began.

"Detective!" Judge Silverstone tried to stop him, but he was too far gone.

How dare this woman talk about my partner in this manner! Cohen thought as he ranted on. "My partner was a good cop! He never once did a crooked thing in his life. Those two bastards right there," he pointed at Dog and Pretty E, "Killed him! They killed my partner!" he said emotionally.

"Bam! Bam! Bam!" the judge's gavel sounded as he slammed it down on the table to take control over the courtroom. "Detective Cohen, you are out of line! Totally out of line! I'm going to ask you to leave the courtroom. That's and order!"

"Your Honor," Lucy cut in. "I'm done with the witness."

"Okay," he replied, then said, "Detective Cohen, you may leave the courtroom," and the detective stomped out of the witness box.

"May I have the Prosecution's closing arguments?" Judge Silverstone asked, satisfied that the trial that went on for hours had finally come to an end.

Judge Silverstone listened to both of the closing arguments from the prosecutor and defense, than called for a recess. He didn't know why, because his decision was already made the minute Detective Cohen went absolutely bananas. They were innocent; he couldn't find one reason within himself that could make him decide beyond a reasonable doubt that they were anything other than innocent. There just wasn't enough evidence. There were no fingerprints on anything, and the money could be accounted for because their businesses made enough income to cover it. Plus, there was motive for him to believe that maybe the drugs were planted on them, and they were actually innocent.

When Judge Silverstone returned to the courtroom from his chambers, each and every spectator, media reporter, bailiff, and police officer was on the edge of their seats anticipating the verdict. He looked out over his courtroom at both the prosecutor and the defense lawyer and began:

"After careful review and consideration of both sides of this case, I've come to the conclusion that beyond a reasonable doubt, I find the defendants, Mr. Michael Lollie and Eric Benson, innocent of all charges," he finished.

"This court is now adjourned!" and the families of both Dog and Pretty E made huge outbursts of, "Thank you, Jesus!" and their joy spread out into the hallway.

Dog jumped up, hugged Pretty E and ran towards the waiting arms of his wife, Kim, while Pretty E turned to Lucy. He gave her a hug and whispered in her ear, "Thank you!" and was truly grateful. Lucy had saved him again, and he'd be forever fond of her for that, not to mention the baby she was carrying for him.

"Listen, baby," he whispered under the noise of the still celebrating people. "I need you to go home. I'll be there in the morning, I promise. Just let me go get Tammy off of my back, make her feel important, because, baby, she knows too much. So much, that if I rubbed her the wrong way and she decided to call the police, not even the late Johnny Cochran could get me off," and she understood.

Chapter Thirteen

Outside of the courthouse, a mob of reporters were posted for comments from Lucy, the lawyer who had just done what the people had started to believe was virtually impossible to do. She beat the incomparable prosecutor, Donavan. They also wanted to hear from the two defendants who had been convicted of being kingpins before they had even gone to trial. That just goes to show that the media isn't always right.

With their loved ones in tow and their lawyer leading the way, they stepped from beyond the courtroom doors right into the center ring of the media circus. Instantly, they were swarmed and almost mangled by the mob as the pictures began snapping and the questions began flying.

"Ms. Vault! When did you decide to switch sides?" one reporter asked.

"Ms. Vault! The people want to know, are you and Eric Benson lovers? If so, why is he with her?" another one asked as a huge flashbulb from a camera flashed and captured a picture of Tammy and Pretty E that would be plastered on the front of tomorrow's newspaper. The image of them smiling together would rest on Lucy's mind for the rest of the day.

"Ms Vault! How does it feel to have just beaten the lead prosecutor, and probably the next governor?" a third one asked.

"I switched sides because it was the right thing for me, and no, we're not lovers. As for me beating the lead prosecutor, I think you should ask *him* how it feels to have just got beaten by the best lawyer around." She answered all of the questions in one whop.

She wanted to go ahead and respond to each and every question the media had to ask her, in fact she had prepared a speech, but the question about Tammy's presence had shut her down. Tammy was everywhere at all the wrong times, and she was the one person standing in the way of her happiness. Lucy wished there was some way to get rid of the thorn in her side, but she knew that was impossible. She did, however, manage to keep her faith that one day everything would be alright. Right now though, the only thing she wanted to do was go lay down in her bed and escape from the world beyond the womb of her covers.

■■■■■■

Tammy heard the questions the press asked Lucy, and smiled when she heard what the other woman implied, because she knew they were referring to her. She looked to Lucy and flashed a smile of all thirty-two teeth before scooting up next to Pretty E even closer than she already was. The move she made did just what Tammy wanted it to do, as she watched the blood inside Lucy's body boil until it turned her white face red. "Bitch!" Tammy said beneath her breath. The instant gratification she received from the act was good, but not enough to make her feel better. She still had to pay Pretty E's ass back for what he had done. The thought of him sleeping with someone was enough for her to feel sick to her stomach, but for it to be a white girl took the cake. *The nerve of this muthafucka!* she continued to think as she saw the potbelly Lucy was lugging around. *I'ma fix his ass! Watch!* she confirmed.

When they reached the outside of the actual courthouse building, the crowd had almost doubled in size. People were everywhere. Pretty E pushed and shoved his way through the people hurriedly but not disrespectfully, as he tried to reach Tammy's car.

"Eric! Eric!" Shouts escaped the mouths of the media, but he didn't stop. Anything they wanted to know had already been revealed in court, so there was no reason for him to tell them anything they already knew. The fact had been proven, they were innocent, and now he just wanted to get away from all the focus. Tomorrow's headlines would be enough information for anyone who wanted to know about what happened in court today.

Tammy tried to stay on Pretty E's heels as he made his way to the car, but somehow she let the media's questions detour her from him.

"Ms., who are you?" one reporter yelled.

"What's your name?" another one shouted.

"Are you Eric's fiancée?" another one asked, and Tammy stopped dead in her tracks. The reporter, who asked the question was an old man whose hair was graying at the edges. Dressed in your reporter's typical plaid blazer, the man looked like a throwback Howard Cosell, but he knew his stuff. He knew that women were emotional, so he drew that card from his stacked deck and dealt it to Tammy. When she picked it up, every media expert and media mogul was in attention, as well as every nosy pedestrian who was outside, drooling at the mouth for something to run off and say to someone who wasn't here.

Tammy heard the word "fiancée" and spun around towards the reporter who asked the question. *Damn right I'm his fiancée!* she thought to herself. *And the world will know after I answer these questions,* she finished.

Tammy walked over to the man in the plaid suit and said, "Yes, I'm his fiancée."

"Ms.—?" he asked her with his eye brows arched.

"Ms. Smith," she answered.

"Ms. Smith, is it true that your fiancé is having an affair with Ms. Jennifer Vault, his attorney?" he asked.

"No, he is not. He never was, and no, it will never be," she answered sternly, cutting her eyes towards Lucy who was surrounded by other reporters.

The keen reporter caught the eyeballing session between the two women and knew there was more to this story, so he threw a curveball into his selection of questions.

"Well, I wouldn't be too sure of that, Ms. Smith, because insiders say that the baby she's carrying belongs to your fiancé," he said, and the remark did exactly what he wanted it to do. It brought Tammy out of her natural character, and she snapped, even if, in fact, everything he had implied turned out to be true, and her reaction made for a juicy article.

"Let me tell you some 'em, you li'l fat bald headed man! You reporters always have some 'em negative to say, or always try to start some shit up! I see why so many of you muthafuckas get knocked out every year!" she said, and stormed off. "Now get the fuck out of my way 'for you be the next reporter knocked out!" she finished, and pushed her way towards her car.

By the time Tammy had finally reached the car, Pretty E was boiling mad. He had to sit in the car for the past twenty minutes, fending off newspaper reporters who had wanted a statement. "Man, where the fuck is this bitch at?" he asked himself, while at the same time telling reporters through a cracked window to back away.

This whole trial thing had drained him mentally. However, it also eased him, because the ten to twenty year sentence he faced if convicted was no longer threatening his life. All he wanted to do now was put this whole thing behind him and move on, but Tammy was holding that up. "I wish she hurry the fuck up!" he said as he saw her break away from the media circus that she allowed to swarm her in front of the courthouse.

As Tammy approached the car, she saw the look on Pretty E's face and knew he was mad, but hell, she was mad too. No matter how much she tried not to think about it, the thoughts of him fucking this white girl, Lucy, would not leave her mind. *Damn, I wonder if he was eatin' dat bitch's pussy? I wonder if he was whispering the same shit in her ear that he whispered in mine,* were just some of the thoughts that roamed in her head.

Tammy got in her car and pulled away from the news reporters who had her car surrounded, and never once even glanced over towards Pretty E as she headed down King Street. She faded over into her far right lane and bent around the curve onto I-95 North, and headed home to Philly.

Pretty E noticed her mood and the way she looked and forgot that he was even mad. "Wha's wrong wit' chu?" he asked, but she didn't answer. "Why you ain't sayin' nuffin'?"

"Because I don't believe you, that's why," she answered.

"What chu talking about?"

"I'm talking about you fuckin' that white bitch, that's what!"

"Yo, why is you buggin'?" He paused, then said, "Why are you still on dat bullshit? I told you that shit wasn't nuffin'."

"Is that your baby?" she asked, but he went silent. "I said, is dat your baby?" she repeated, but this time she demanded an answer.

"I don't know. There's a possibility that it could be," he answered, and the tears began to fall from her eyes.

"Are you alright?" he asked, as heavy sobs escaped her from deep down within her soul, but there was no way to heal it. The cut was too deep, and it hurt really badly. No medicine in the world could heal what she was feeling, and there wasn't a bandage in existence that could cover the wound. It would have to heal on its own. For now though, revenge was on her mind and payback was her motive, and she had the perfect plan.

■■■■■■

In nearly no time, Tammy was crossing the Pennsylvania State line, going into Philly. She still hadn't said one word since the moment Pretty E told her that he might be the father of the child Lucy was carrying. She did, however, occasionally nod her head to her new Destiny's Child CD that played loudly in her car system. There was something about the disc that gave her strength. In all reality though, it just simply reminded her to tap into the inner strength she already possessed.

Tammy got off of I-95 at the Callowhill Street exit, and drove into North Philly where she lived. She drove down Broad Street, taking the scenic route down Allegheny Avenue, where she made a left to head home. When she made it down to 28th Street and parked in front of her row home, she was glad she had taken the scenic route. It had given her a chance to see and recognize just how beautiful the City of Brotherly Love could actually be. From the new football stadium built for the Eagles, to the Liberty Bell, clean down to the graffiti on the walls of the streets, Philadelphia was her home and she loved it.

"So you still ain't going to say nuffin'?" Pretty E asked.

"Yeah, what do you want me to say?" she asked gingerly, as if she was never mad.

"Yo, wha's up? Why you be switchin' up so much? One minute you mad, the next minute you smiling and shit. Wha's up wit' dat?"

"Wha's up wit' what?"

"Never mind," he said to himself, as he followed her into the house.

Mmm-hmm, he thinks I forgot, don't he? I told him he's going to get his. I'ma rock his ass right to sleep, and fuck him up for playing games with me. Watch! she told herself, then asked him, "Baby, are you hungry?" in that soft and sexy tone he loved so much.

"Yeah, fix me some 'em to eat, please," he answered.

"What chu want?"

"I don't care, whatever you make I'ma eat."

"You want a steak?"

"Yeah, bring me a steak. That'll hit the spot."

Pretty E flopped down on the couch and grabbed the remote to the television. He flipped from channel to channel aimlessly until he thought he passed Dog on the screen, then flicked backwards until he found the station. His eyes hadn't lied. Dog and Lucy were on television surrounded by news reporters, and then a commercial came on. With that, he kicked off his shoes, got comfortable on the couch, and looked at his watch. He saw that his timepiece read 5:27 p.m. and realized that was the end of the first segment of news. The next showing was at 5:30.

When the news started again, the top story was the innocent verdict handed down by the judge at the trial of two alleged drug kingpins in Wilmington, Delaware. The anchorman went on to explain further into detail about how the police arrested him and Dog, then had the allegations of them being connected to the Mob, and showed flashes of Frankie and Joey walking out of the courthouse.

"That's the boss of the Capelli family shown here in the white, and here's a picture of reputed Mob under boss, Joey (The Fox) Vito in the blue," the anchorman said while their pictures were being shown.

Damn! Pretty E thought as he was actually on the news making the headlines. "I see what Rasul was talking about now," he said out loud as he reflected on some of the talks they'd had up to this point.

Everything Rasul had told him up to this point had gone in one ear and out the other, until now. He never really took the conversations they had seriously, because he looked at himself as the same old Pretty E. Damn the fact that he was a millionaire who owned businesses and stocks, because none of that mattered to him. He was still Eric at heart, and wasn't going to change for anyone.

Now, as he watched how he was portrayed on the news and looked at how Rasul had changed, he realized that Rasul hadn't changed at all. He just grew up and took on the role of an adult. He realized that they were under a microscope, and were known by the police and the people in their neighborhoods, so it was time to change and get smart. *Damn, maybe it is time to change, fall, back, and leave the game alone,"* he thought as Tammy brought him his plate.

"Here, baby," she said, and held the steak, potato, and broccoli out to him on the plate. "Here, let me go get your salad. What kind of dressing you want?"

"Thousand Island," he said as she walked off.

Tammy sat across from Pretty E and watched him eat his food. He had fallen right into her trap of paying him back, and he didn't even know it. The only thing she had to do now was wait. She watched as he shoveled fork after forkful of the meal she cooked him down his throat, and wondered if her plan would work. She knew he would drink the juice, but would the three Zanax she put in his drink kick in when her cousin said they would? She didn't know, but she did know her cousin, Li'l Larry, wouldn't lie to her. He had been taking Zanax for years, along with a syrup he drank from down off of 18th and Masters that the hustlers called "their drink".

"I'm telling you, cousin," Li'l Larry said, then continued. "These mu'fuckas right here are goin' to put him on his ass in about a half hour to forty five minutes, I'm telling you," he assured her.

I sure hope so, she thought as she crushed the little blue pills up into powder and mixed them in his juice. It didn't matter to her one way or another how fast the pills worked, as long as they worked.

When he finally picked up the juice she set before him, she stared so hard that he became suspicious. "What chu looking at?" he asked with a smile on his face, then stared at the cup he held in his hand. "Girl you ain't put nuffin' in my drink did you?" he asked jokingly, but was dead serious.

"Boy, why would I put some 'em in your drink? Do you really think I would do some 'em like that? Because if you do, you don't need to be with me," she said.

"I'm just playing, baby. You know I'm just playing," he said, and thought, *Yeah, why would she do that,* and tossed the cup back.

Tammy stood up and walked over to where he sat and began to clean up after him. She grabbed the empty plate, paper towel, and glass of ice cubes and headed off to the kitchen. "Baby, you want anything else?" she yelled

"Nah, I'm straight."

"Alright," she said, and put the dishes in the sink.

After returning from the kitchen, she walked over and sat next to Pretty E, positioning herself for the second part of her plan. She let her hand fall down to his knee and work itself up and down his leg, as she inched up closer to him.

"Baby," she asked softly. "Do you love me?"

"Yeah, I love you. Why would you ask me something like that right now?"

"Because I'm just making sure, that's all."

"Sure for what?" he asked, still on point from earlier. He hadn't forgotten how strange she was acting.

"For nuffin', boy. I just like to know sometimes, being that you don't say it that much. So, tell me," she said and rubbed his toy in between his legs.

"I love you, Tammy."

"I love you too. Come on, let's go take a shower, make love, and just hold each other for the rest of the night. Don't that, sound good?"

"Mmm-hmm," he moaned, more focused on her hand than on her question as she stood up to head upstairs

■■■■■■

The shower water was steaming hot, but not to the point where you couldn't stand under it. Tammy stood right up under the spout and washed herself, taking her time on her most intimate spots. She used the bath sponge to erotically rub along her breasts, causing her nipples to become hard, as Pretty E stood watching with his mouth open.

It had been a long time since she had put on a show like this for him, and he loved it. Tammy was good at this, because she was so sexy. Plus, she could dance. He still believed deep down in his heart that she used to dance before they met, because some of her closest friends were dancers. But that didn't matter. Tammy was the love of his life. He watched the way she moved, the way she licked her lips and stared at him seductively, and he felt himself becoming erect. He walked up to her until they were chest to breasts, and they kissed passionately as the water beat down their bodies. He wanted her, needed to feel her.

Tammy reached down and stroked his love muscle with her hand, but Pretty E pulled away. "Wha's wrong?" she asked.

"Nuffin'," he replied. "I just want to be in control today, so let me do this," he said, and dropped to his knees. "Here," he said, grabbing her leg. "Put your foot up here," and she followed his lead.

Tammy placed her foot up on the faucet and he placed his face right where she was shaved, and greedily ate away from the back. He rubbed, pulled, smacked, and squeezes at her ass, while his tongue flickered in and out of her pussy and ass. *Damn!* Tammy thought, as she shuttered and jumped from time to time at the feeling she was getting.

"Do it feel good, baby?" he managed to ask between licks.

"Yeah, baby! Yeah! It feels real good!" she moaned, and placed her hands on the walls for balance as she came back to back in his mouth. "Oooooh, baby! Yeah, baby! Right there!" she screamed from the orgasm.

Tammy's body was still trembling, but she managed to cock her ass up in the air anyway. "Here, baby, put it in," she said in almost a begging manner, but he ignored the request.

Pretty E stood up and cut the shower water off, then stepped out of the tub. Tammy was puzzled at first until he stood at the side and reached in to pick her up. He carried her into the bedroom, and she grabbed a towel from the door on the way in because their bodies were still wet. She threw it across the bed to protect the comforter and sheets from getting wet, and then he lay her down. He climbed on top of her and they kissed as they rolled around over the towel until he was lying on his back.

Tammy smiled, then kissed him softly as she worked her way down towards his toy, only stopping to let her tongue tickle his softest spots. She bit at his nipples, nibbled at his skin, and sucked passion marks all over his body. When she reached his toy, she didn't use any hands. She went at it mouth first, letting her tongue flip it into her mouth. Moving her neck back and forth, she allowed him to slide smoothly in and out of mouth, making him cringe from the feeling. "Sssss! Damn, baby, that shit feels good!"

"Do it?" she slurped.

"Mmm-hmm!"

Tammy continued to work her mouth until he was fully erect, then she climbed on top of him. She grabbed his toy from beneath her and positioned it so she could sit down on it. Once it was aimed in the right direction, she eased her body down onto it and began to work her hips. Up and down she bounced, feeling him plunge deep inside of her as little moans of both pleasure and pain escaped her mouth. The more she bounced and ground her hips, the more he squirmed underneath her power, until she began to feel his body locking up. She knew what was about to happen, so she worked her hips faster, trying to bring herself to a climax with him. She was right at the brink of exploding when she got some help form the hot burst of liquid that shot up inside her from his manhood, and she screamed, "Oh my God! I'm cumming!" as she sat all the way down on him and soaked his stomach and pubic hairs with both of their juices.

Tammy got up and stood on the side of the bed, and used the towel to dab at the juices that still oozed from her body. She looked down at Pretty E to see if the drugs were working yet, and they must have been, because she could see him fighting his sleep. Her plan was working.

The only qualms she had about the whole thing now was that she didn't know whether she could go through with it or not. She loved him too much to kill him in his sleep, but he had scorned her—crushed her world to oblivion. *He has to feel some pain,* she reasoned with herself as she watched him fall into a deep sleep.

Tammy crept out of the room and headed downstairs to the kitchen. She looked under the sink and grabbed the largest pot she had under there, which was her greens pot, and began to fill it with water. She turned the stove's burner to high and placed the pot on top of it and watched as the flames tickled the bottom.

"You are going to pay for what you've done to me," she kept telling herself regarding Pretty E, fueling her rage even more.

She walked over to the cabinets and grabbed the bottle of syrup and poured the whole thing of Ms. Butterworth's into the hot water, and watched it began to boil together. *This shit is going to stick to his ass,* she thought as the liquid bubbled.

Tammy grabbed two potholders and turned the fire off to pick up the pot from the stove. Carefully but quickly, she climbed the stairs, trying not to splash the hot lava-like water on herself, and entered the bedroom. She stood at the foot of the bed and began to cry as she hovered over his naked body.

"I'm sorry, baby, but you hurt me for the last time," she said, and threw the water.

His screams were deafening.

Chapter Fourteen

Rasul was glad to have finally put the whole thing behind him. He was ready to move forward with his life on some legal shit. The trial was the only thing keeping him from doing so, but now that was over. There was nothing else connecting him to the game. It was over... *hopefully,* he thought.

"They see things the way I'm seeing them, because we're hot as a muthafucka. These crackers got their eyes on us. The next time they jam us up on some shit, we ain't walking. Them mu'fuckas going to give us life in the joint, and I ain't goin' out like dat," he said to himself, and his thoughts were broken up by Tameeka.

"Baby, it's almost that time," she said.

"Time for what?" he asked

"Time for me to have the baby. My due date is in four days."

"I know that. I thought you was talking about some 'um else."

"Well, aren't you happy?"

"What chu think?" he asked, and went to hug her as she lay on the couch. "Damn right I'm happy!"

"Oh!" she said, satisfied. "Did you come up with a name yet?"

"I don't know. If it's a boy, I want to name him after me. If it's a girl, I want to name her Taquila."

"Eeewww, boy! No! Hell no, we ain't naming my baby no Taquila. We gonna name her Ocean."

"Ocean?"

"Yeah, Ocean. Don't you like that?"

"Yeah, I like that. It's unique. I don't think I've ever heard that before."

"That's what I'm sayin'. I only know one girl name Ocean, and I said that if I ever had a daughter, that was going to be her name."

"Okay, we're going to name her Ocean then," he said.

Then his phone rang. He grabbed the phone from the clip on his side and looked at the number. He really didn't want to answer it, because he was spending quality time with his wife and stepson, but it was Frankie. "Hello!" he answered, then remembered he wasn't done with the game.

"Hello, Rasul?"

"Yeah, wha's up, Frankie?"

"Nothing much over here. How's Tameeka doing? Is everything okay?"

"Yeah, everything's fine."

"I'm glad to see that the boys made out today, huh? That Lucy broad sure is good."

"Yeah, she's very good."

"Ain't it a shame?"

"For what?"

"That she has to go so soon," he said, and Rasul went silent. He knew the day was coming when he would have to handle his business, but he wasn't expecting it to come so soon. He was at least expecting a few days, maybe even weeks, but by the way this phone conversation was going, it looked like it might be going down tonight. *Damn!* he thought. *How am I going to kill this broad, knowing that my boy loves her? Plus, she's carrying his baby,* he said to himself in a apologetic manner, as if to apologize for even entertaining the thought. He knew Pretty E was going to be heartbroken, and would never be able to forgive him for doing it. That's why he knew once the act was committed, it would be something else that he would have to take to the grave with him.

"What do you mean 'so soon'?"

"I mean, it's time for you to take care of your end of the deal. The trial is over."

"I know, but…"

"But the trial is over. Handle the business, Rasul, tonight. Or, I can send my guys, and then I'd be upset because you didn't keep your word."

"Alright, Frankie, I get the point."

"Tell Tameeka that my wife and I send our hello's."

"I sure will."

"Okay, bye, and I'll see you tomorrow."

"Okay, see you then," Rasul replied, and the phone went dead.

Rasul put the phone back into its clip and went back to entertaining his wife and stepson, but he couldn't concentrate on just that any longer. The time had finally come for him to kill Lucy, and he was having second thoughts. His heart wasn't as cold as it used to be. Besides, Lucy had become a close friend to him since coming back to defend his friends at the trial, and he had forgiven her on more than one occasion. Yes, her past followed her, and what she did would never be forgotten, but she was forgiven in his book. He had done that the day she cried to him for nearly and hour, sincerely apologizing for the death of Hit-Man. She was only doing her job as a federal agent, but Frankie would never understand that part. The only thing in the world worse than a cop was a snitch, but pigs were pigs. Once a pig always a pig, just like leopards couldn't change their spots. They would always be leopards.

Tameeka felt the vibe from her husband turn sour, and knew that something about the phone call was bothering him. She'd been around him too long not to have known. She sat up on the couch and leaned up against him and rubbed the back of his neck, while he rested his head in the palms of his hands, letting his fingers massage his temples. "You alright, baby?" she asked.

"Yeah, I'm cool. I'll just be so glad when I'm able to just relax when it's all over. I don't know what to do."

"It is over, isn't it?" she asked.

"Yeah, after tonight. I got one more thing to take care of, and then we're just going to make more babies, you hear me? I want five more," he said, smiling and trying to change the mood.

"I don't know about five, but we'll definitely try for two," she said honestly.

"Two's good enough. Now, come on upstairs and go to bed," he said, and turned to Jaquaan. "Yo, we're goin to finish our shit up tomorrow, okay?"

"Yeah, Dad, that's wha's up!"

"Yo man, what I tell you about that? You don't' have to call me Dad if you don't want to."

"But I want to."

"I heard that!" Rasul said, and the feeling was gratifying.

■■■■■■

153

Rasul looked over at the clock and decided to get up. It was one thirty in the morning, and it couldn't have been a better time to move if he had planned it. It was actually the perfect time to move, because everyone was normally inside and sleeping, and the streets were real quiet, especially out on Route 40.

Rasul got up and walked to the walk-in closet and pulled the string that hung oddly from the ceiling, and the light came on. *That's a damn shame,* he thought as he looked around the huge closet and saw nothing but his wife's clothes and shoes. "Damn, look at my shit!" he said, chuckling under his breath at the little bit of space he had. It couldn't have been any larger than a tenth of the closet, but he was alright with it.

He flipped through his little wardrobe, and in no time found what he was looking for. He grabbed the black Jordan sweatsuit and put it on right there in the middle of the closet, then reached in a old Timberland box and grabbed his nine millimeter before slipping into his black Air Ones. He turned and looked in the mirror for self-approval and nodded his head. He was ready.

Rasul turned the light off and stepped from beyond the closet doors and back into the bedroom, carrying the steel in his hand low at his side. He grabbed his black-onblack Sixers fitted hat and pulled it down over his eyebrows like Jadakiss, then placed the gun in his jacket pocket.

"Baby, what are you doing? Where do you think you're going at 1:37 in the morning?" Tameeka asked, flicking on the light at her bedside, and then sitting up with her back against the headboard.

"I told you I gotta handle some business."

"Well, can't it wait until tomorrow?"

"No, I gotta handle it now. It'll only take about an hour, and I'll be right back."

"I don't think you should go."

"Why not?"

"'Cause I gotta funny feeling."

"Why do you always do that? The last time you said to stay with you and I left, I got a mu'fuckin' speeding ticket. What you trying to do, jinx me or some 'um?"

"Why would I jinx you? That would be stupid, right? Because if something was to happen to you, I wouldn't have you here with me. All I'm sayin' is, when I tell you something, just listen. The last time I said come on, let's go on vacation, look what happened. Dog and Pretty E got locked up. So don't say I'm trying to jinx you when I'm really only looking out."

"Look, baby. I don't feel like arguing, nor do I want to fight. Let me go handle my business so I can get back, okay?" he said, and she sat there with her lips poked out. "Quit acting like a baby. I'll be right back."

■■■■■■

Tameeka couldn't go back to sleep if she tried; not now anyway. Something bad was about to happen, she could feel it. She got out of bed and raced to the window, only to see the tail lights of her Range Rover escaping around the corner of her development. She had to stop him some kind of way from doing whatever it was he was about to do, but how? That was the problem. The fear of what was about to go down was so stressful to her that she began to shake. Her nerves were crazy, so she tried to sit.

Then it happened. Her water broke and a pain she had never felt before shot through her body. "Oh shit! What was that?" she asked herself in a panic, and clutched her belly. She didn't remember a pain like that when she was carrying Jaquaan.

Then it happened again. "Oh my God! Something is wrong!" she told herself, then at the top of her voice, she called Jaquaan. "Baby, hurry up! Come and take me to the hospital!" she screamed.

■■■■■■

Rasul made it all the way out to Route 7 in about fifteen minutes. That was good, coming from out of the city in which it usually took nearly thirty to forty-five minutes to get there. He made it that fast because the highway was nearly empty. He got off at Route 7 because he wanted to take the back road to Route 40. He didn't want to take any chances on passing by a police officer that might be lingering in the cut and waiting to pull a nigga over. Plus, Route 40 was the way he wanted to take back to the highway after leaving the bloody scene. He came to that conclusion because he figured this would be the route the police would be taking when they were called to the scene, and he'd be leaving the scene, so they'd be passing each other instead of running into each other.

Rasul made a left into the Fox Run Apartment Complex and parked nearly three buildings away. He made up his next moves as he went along. "I'ma call her on my phone, tell her to open the door, then I'ma put two in her. One in her head and one in her gut. Then, I'ma grab her cell phone, take her purse and leave the scene. In and out, that's all it is," he talked to himself as he neared the building. He dialed all of the numbers to Lucy's phone except for the last one, and then his phone rang in his hand. "Hello!" he answered.

"Dad, Mom is having the baby!" Jaquaan said, and Rasul's heart dropped into his stomach.

"Okay, look. I'm on my way! Who's there?"

"Nobody yet, but Tammy and Pretty E are on their way. So is Grandma and them."

"Why they comin'?" he asked, then thought to himself, *They probably want some money.*

"They said they wanted to be here, that's all."

"Alright, I'm on my way."

As soon as his phone disconnected, he called Dog. He didn't want to call him, because he knew that he was spending time with his family celebrating the trial victory, but he had to tell him. He wanted him to share his joy with him, and just like he thought, Dog said, "Me and Kim are on our way!"

Then after that call, Rasul called his mother and grandmother, saving the call to Frankie for last. Tameeka's going into labor couldn't have come at a better time, because now he didn't have to kill Lucy. It gave him more time to think and try to come up with a way to save her life, but he knew that was farfetched.

"Hello!" Frankie said, still more than half sleep.

"Frankie, get up! Tameeka's having the baby!" he yelled into the phone, nearly giving Frankie a heart attack. "Come on, man! You're about to be a Pop-Pop! Now meet me at the hospital."

"Are you for real? I'm about to be a Pop-Pop?"

"Yeah, now get your ass out here! I'll handle the business later on."

"To hell with the business right now! I'm about to be a Pop-Pop again! You just get out there to that hospital and I'll meet you there in a few minutes."

"Alright, I'll see you then," he said, and started running back to the Range Rover.

■■■■■■

When the water hit the wall, it splashed in nearly every direction. Tammy just couldn't bring herself to throw it directly on him, but what did hit him had caused just as much damage. The hot lava-like mixture had landed on his chest and whole left side, causing him to scream in agony. His screams were so high-pitched and filled with pain that she dropped the pot to cover her ears.

"Oh my God! Baby, I'm so sorry!" she cried, but he couldn't hear her, because the pain too excruciating for him to concentrate on anything other than the pain.

Pretty E couldn't stop screaming, or he just didn't want to. Somehow, the more he screamed, the less pain he felt, so he hollered at the top of his lungs. He really didn't know what was happening to him, because he was coming out of a serious drug nod. However, when he finally did gain some sense and saw Tammy standing over top him, he jumped up. With everything he had left in his body, he lunged at her and swung with all his might.

Tammy saw the forceful blow coming, but ducked in the nick of time, only catching a graze of the blow on top of the head.

"Bitch, I'ma kill ya ass!" he snapped as he landed on top of her and continued to swing. Pretty E swung every blow in a manner that would have torn her head off if they connected, but she was balled up in the fetal position, defending herself.

If the pain hadn't come back when it did, he would have been still throwing blows, but it felt like he was on fire. Pretty

E jumped up, ran to the bathroom, and turned on the sink to splash some cold water on his burns. That was the worst thing he could have ever done, because the water peeled his skin off to the pink meat.

"AAAAAAHHH!" he shouted, and sucked air through his teeth. "Bitch! What da fuck is wrong with you! AAAAAAHHH! I'ma fuck you up! Word, I'ma fuck you up!"

"Baby, I'm sorry! I'm so sorry, baby!" she pleaded, and she really was sorry as she saw the pink meat on his chest.

"Oh, hell no, bitch! Sorry can't save your ass now!" he said, and gave her a look that sent chills up her spine.

Tammy was terrified when he looked over his shoulder at her while he stood before the sink. His eyes were piercing and cold, looking as if the Pretty E she had known had left the body of the man standing in her bathroom. For the first time in their three year relationship, she had seen what so many people had said about her man long ago, but she denied the accusations. Pretty E was a cold-blooded killer when he transformed. His eyes told her so, and she was literally shaken by the thought.

"Bitch," he said. "You threw water on the right muthafucka! That's the last time you throw anything else, bitch, I can promise you that. I should cut your muthafuckin' hands off, you stupid bastard!"

Tammy couldn't believe her ears. She couldn't believe he was talking to her like that. His words hurt almost more than anything he could have done physically to her, because they were his true thoughts coming out aloud. *He can't feel that way about me, can he?* she asked herself, and was saved by the phone ringing.

"Hello!" Tammy answered.

"Aunt Tammy, my mom is about to have the baby!" Jaquaan said. "Are y'all coming?"

"Yeah, we're on our way, baby. Tell your mom don't have dat until we get there, okay?"

"Okay," he answered, and she hung up the phone. Tammy tip-toed back over to the bathroom door, and as softly as she could she said, "Baby, Tameeka is about to have the baby and everybody wants us to come."

"She is?" he asked, and for a split second he forgot about the pain.

"Yeah!"

"Well, come on then, 'cause I gotta go to the hospital anyway," he said, looking at his burns in the mirror. "You might need to see a doctor too, 'cause I'ma fuck you up. I might fuck you up every time I look at dis shit!" he said, and grabbed his keys. "Here, you drive," he continued, tossing her the keys.

"Alright," she said, and they left Philly.

Chapter Fifteen

The waiting room in the Christiana Hospital in Stanton Delaware had become more of a panic room than a lobby, after the doctor said what he said and the hours rolled by.

Tammy and Kim had a nervous look on their faces, and so did Tameeka's mother and grandmother. Rasul's mom was comforting Jaquaan, but even she was beginning to worry with every tick of the clock.

Dog, Pretty E, and Frankie were more relaxed than worried. Their views were optimistic about the whole thing, because they were in a hospital. *If anything did go wrong, at least they were here,* was the thought that kept them calm. Plus, they were still joking on Pretty E about the bandage that could be seen up around his neck.

"I told you, nigga. You keep playin' with these broads, one of 'em was going to fuck you up," Dog said.

"How about it?" Frankie added. "See, Pretty E, what happened to you happened because you really don't know how to play. Now back in my day, I was what you called a… let's say, a 'charmer'. I treated all my women the same. All except the one I married. If I brought one, I brought the other. It was just that simple, and no one had anything to say because they knew their position. Now, what *you* do is you play with 'em. You run around and tell all of them that they're the one. You can't do that, because that's a lie. That's why you're sitting here all burned up now, because emotions cause people to do some crazy shit, and that's just one of them. You're lucky she didn't kill you."

"I wish she would'a. I would'a fucked her ass up!" Pretty E said seriously.

"A dead man ain't never hurt nobody," Frankie replied, and they all broke out into laughter.

■■■■■■

Rasul stood at Tameeka's bedside holding her hand, but they both were speechless. What the doctor had told them before he left to inform their people was still fresh on their minds, because they had to make a decision. The baby was in a breech position so oddly that her uterus was in danger of collapsing. If that happened, she could die, so the decision had to be made. They were either going to keep the baby or terminate it, but they had to decide fast, because they were running out of time. The choice was life or death on both sides of the decision, and that's what made it so hard to decide. The doctor said that if they decided to keep the baby, there was a 50/50 chance that Tameeka would live after the birth. However, there was still that 50/50 chance that she might die. The only sure thing was that she would live if they terminated the baby.

"Baby, what are we going to do?" Rasul asked, showing a sign of weakness to her for the first time she'd known him.

"We're going to have this baby, that's what we're going to do," Tameeka said confidently.

"I don't know, baby. The doctor said..." Rasul tried to say but was cut off.

"Fuck what the doctor said! This is our decision, and I say we're going to have our baby. I carried it too long now not to have it. We are going to be fine, baby. Do you hear me? Look at me," she said, pulling him close to her. "I'm going to be alright, and so is the baby. I delivered Jaquaan and his big headed ass, didn't I?" She didn't wait for an answer before continuing. "Well, I can deliver this one too."

"Are you sure?" he asked, questioning his own better judgment.

"Baby, I ain't never been so sure," she lied, and began to pray a silent prayer.

Tameeka wasn't sure if she was making the right decision or not, but she was sure not going to kill this baby inside of her, and she didn't care what anyone would have said. This baby that she was carrying was alive and well inside of her body. It was her job as a mother not only make a decision for herself, but for this child too. Now, if the doctors had known all the possibilities when she was early in her pregnancy, then maybe she would have had an abortion. The baby inside of her now was fully developed and ready for the world, and all she could do now was see its little eyes, visualize its toothless smile, and its little fingers and toes. *If I was early on in my pregnancy, yeah, I could have terminated it, but not now,* she thought.

Tameeka looked over at her beautiful husband in every way, and gave him the biggest, brightest smile she could muster up and said, "Baby, give me a kiss, then tell me you love me."

"I love you," he said, staring in the same gray eyes that captivated him years ago.

"Promise me you'll never leave me," she said.

"I promise."

"Baby, I love you. You are the best thing that could have happened to me and Jaquaan, and I want to say thank you. Now, get the doctor, and let's do this."

■■■■■■

The doctor wheeled Tameeka into the delivery room and induced her labor to take some of the pressure off of her uterus and help ease the delivery. With in minutes, her uterus was dilated to ten centimeters, the correct size to deliver, and the doctor told her to push.

Tameeka was careful when she did so, because she remembered what the doctor said. Too much pressure or strain on her uterus could cause it to collapse, and she could bleed to death, so she pushed slow and easy. Sweat beaded upon her forehead, and she took deep and heavy breaths through her nose, letting it out through her mouth, as she looked to Rasul.

"Yeah, baby! Like dat! You're doing great!" he said, excited as he coached her on.

"Just a few more pushes, Mrs. Jefferies. I can see the head," the doctor instructed.

"Okay!" Tameeka said, and pushed again. This time she felt her vagina split, and the doctor pulling the baby out of her.

"What is it?" she asked, relieved that the delivery had been successful. *Thank you, Jesus!* she said to herself, and rested her head back on the pillow.

"It's a girl! It's a girl baby!" Rasul shouted happily, and those words would be the last words she would ever hear again in this lifetime.

She tried to sit up, but she couldn't. She tried to speak, but her mouth wouldn't move. Her body had become warm, and a sensational feeling shot through her body. It sort of felt like she was having an orgasm, but she wasn't. It was the only other thing she could think of that felt this good, but even that feeling couldn't compare.

What's happening to me? she asked herself. *Why ain't I moving? Rasul, what's wrong with me?* she asked, but he didn't respond. He was too busy cutting the umbilical cord and standing with out-stretched arms, waiting for the doctor to pass him the baby.

Then it hit her. She was at the top of the room looking down on the whole scene. *Oh my God!* she thought. *I'm dead!* But it wasn't a panic. In fact, she was at peace and feeling better than she had ever felt before. There was no pain, and she knew deep down inside that everything was going to be fine with her husband and kids, so she didn't even try to fight. She had given up on this lifetime effortlessly, and was in the spiritual aspect of life now. That person lying on the table was just a shell now, however, she was still alive and well. Tameeka smiled when the angels that stood on both sides of her grabbed her hands to take her away.

"Bye, baby! I love you, okay? Always remember that," she said, but he'd never know it. It would be a question he'd ask himself for many years to come.

■■■■■■

Rasul yelled, "It's a girl!" at the top of his lungs, and Tammy, along with the rest of the family in the waiting room, was on her way to the delivery room.

He grabbed the scissors from the doctor, cut the umbilical cord, and the little girl screamed to life. He held his arms out for the doctor to lay her in them, and he rocked her gently. "Shhh, don't cry Mom-Mom, Daddy got you," he said, but his words meant nothing. The baby screamed, kicked, and grabbed at the air with her little hands spread open, while keeping her eyes closed tightly. Her little comfort zone she acquired while in her mother's womb had been penetrated, and the new experience was frightening for the bundle of joy.

The baby had a head full of hair, and was dark chocolate already, so Rasul knew she was going to be dark like Tameeka, if not darker.

Rasul looked over to Tameeka lying back with her eyes closed and instantly felt uneasy. *Why isn't she looking at what's going on? How can she be sleep with all this commotion going on?* he asked himself as the family entered the room excitedly. He turned around to Tammy, the first one through the door, and handed her the baby.

"Wha's wrong?" she asked when she saw the blank expression on his face, but he didn't answer. He was focused on Tameeka.

"Meek-Meek, get up, baby! Please! Don't you do this to me, girl! You said we was going to be alright! Come on, baby! Get up! Please, wake up!" he shouted as tears began to find his face. "Doc! Come on, man, do some 'em!" he said, and the doctor asked everyone to clear the room.

"Come on everybody," the nurse began. "The doctor needs everyone out," she finished as she escorted everyone from the room. "That means you too, Mr. Jefferies."

"I'm not going no mu'fuckin' where!" he shouted.

"Please, Mr. Jefferies," she asked again. The doctors need room to work."

"Come on, baby!" his mother yelled from the doorway.

"I'm not going no mu'fuckin' where! Not until I know Meek-Meek is alright, so please, leave me the fuck alone and get out!"

"That means you too, Mr. Jefferies," a doctor said, trying to do what the nurse couldn't do.

"Didn't you just hear what I said, muthafucka? I ain't going anywhere! Now start helping the rest of those doctors out before they be working on your punk ass!" he demanded and stood right there.

After that comment, the doctor walked away. He went over to the table where Tameeka lay and began to work along with the other doctors. With every minute that went by, Rasul began to worry a little more. He watched as they placed an oxygen mask over her face, and stuck an IV in her arm. Then after that, they pulled out a heart defibrillator, containing the electric pads that looked like suction cups, except they were metal.

"Clear!" the doctor holding the pads shouted, and placed them onto her chest. He pressed down on them and zapped Tameeka, causing her body to jump up off the table, but nothing happened, and the heart monitor displayed a straight line.

"Clear!" he said again, and still there was nothing. One more time, and again, nothing happened, but the doctors kept working.

Rasul couldn't believe what was happening. He was powerless, and there was nothing else he could do but watch as the doctors tried to save her life, and that's what made him cry harder. His once little grunts had become loud sobs. They were so deep and filled with grief that the nurse at his side began to cry. She had never seen a man hurt so deep. She did know this, though. If she could cry just as the man standing next to her by just empathizing, she could imagine how he felt.

When the doctor in charge hung his head and turned around to face him, he already knew what it was. The doctor walked straight over to him, looked him in the eyes and said, "I'm sorry, Mr. Jefferies, but Mrs. Jefferies is no longer with us."

Rasul screaming of the words "Nooooooo!" could still be heard in the ears of every person in that room today if they closed their eyes and thought about it. He could no longer stand. His legs had given way and he slid down in the corner and just cried.

Meek-Meek was gone, and so was a piece of his soul.

■■■■■■

They heard the scream and all began crying at the same time. They didn't need for the doctor or Rasul to come and tell them what had happened, because Rasul's scream said it all. Tameeka was gone.

Pretty E and Dog were the first to rise from their seats. They weren't crying as loud as everyone else was, but tears had fallen from their eyes, and even Frankie was teary-eyed. Their main concern now was the wellbeing of Rasul. He needed them right now, and they knew it.

Frankie stood up and left the waiting room with Pretty E and Dog, and headed down the hallway to where Tameeka's room was. As soon as they turned the corner, they saw a doctor pushing a hospital bed with a body on it, covered with a sheet, and knew it was Tameeka. Their hearts went out to her. When they entered the room, Rasul jumped up form the corner and ran over to them, fell into their arms and sobbed.

"It's going to be alright," Pretty E assured him.

"Yeah, baby boy. You gotta be strong for that baby girl and Jaquaan," Dog said.

"I know man," Rasul sobbed. "I know, but I'ma miss Meek-Meek. I need Meek-Meek, man!" he cried harder.

"I know, man. We're all are going to miss her. But God wanted her more than we needed her. Let's just be happy that she ain't had to suffer," Pretty E said, and Frankie stepped in.

"Hey, son, come here," Frankie said, putting his arm around Rasul's shoulder blades. "Listen here. You're blessed. You're alive and you're healthy. You had the last past, what? Two or three years with a Godsend. Tameeka was his gift to you, Rasul. She loved you, and she gave you life in the form of that little girl who needs to be held by her daddy right now. Tameeka has served her purpose to you for God, and no one has been to pick her up and hold her yet. Reason being, because everyone was so worried about you's two. Remember Tameeka from who and what she was, then be thankful to God for sending her to you. She has changed you into a man, Rasul. She's the reason you are who you are today. I even see that. That's why I always spoke so highly of her, because I knew she was the one for you. Now tighten up, son. Get yourself together, and go get that little girl."

The nurse that was in the room while Frankie, Dog, and Pretty E comforted Rasul, walked him and Jaquaan down to the nursery, while everyone else followed. Jaquaan was still crying, but Rasul assured him that everything was going to be alright. They had just lost a mother, sister, wife, and best friend all wrapped up in one, but they also gained a lifetime of memories and a gift that will last forever.

The nurse let them into the nursery and sat them down on the couch while she went to get the baby. The family stayed out in the hallway and gave them some time to be alone. It was just them now, Rasul, Jaquaan and the baby. The nurse came back with the little chocolate baby bundled up in a pink blanket and handed her to Rasul. He peeled the cover back away from her face, and she was asleep with her two middle fingers in her mouth.

Jaquaan reached over and pulled her little hand down from her mouth and she frowned her face up. "Look at her," he said as she sucked air until she realized nothing was there. "Doesn't she look just like my mom did?" he asked, and started crying again.

"Yeah, she looks just like her," Rasul said through a cracked voice, as he continued to mess with her. "Wake up, Mom-Mom," he said and tickled her cheeks.

The baby frowned her face up even more the more he messed with her, until she finally woke up. When she flipped her lids open and began to cry, Rasul and Jaquaan really fell apart. Her eyes were gray. She was Tameeka all over again.

"Yo, Dad, what's her name?" Jaquaan asked.

"Tameeka Ocean Jefferies," he replied. "Meek-Meek."

Chapter Sixteen

Lucy drove home from her prenatal care appointment rather quickly today, because it was almost time for Pretty E to wake up.

For the past couple of weeks she had been tending to him daily, as if he was her personal patient, and she was loving it. Tammy throwing that water on him was probably the best thing that could have happened to her, because it allowed them some well needed time between the two of them. The incident had brought them closer than they'd ever been before. It had given her a chance to know Pretty E inside and out, and he learned her vise versa. He was a good person all the way down to his soul. He was smart, sexy, and a thug all wrapped up in one. He was just what the doctor ordered for any woman looking for a good bad guy.

They should have cloned him, was Lucy's thought on more than one occasion, and she could see now why Tammy did what she couldn't. She just wouldn't have been able to do it. A little smack for Lucy, or a spit in the face would have been sufficient enough revenge for her. The boiling water or anything that would have caused serious damage to him was totally out of the question. She was an ex-cop, so in no way would she have risked herself being charged with any kind of assault.

When Lucy pulled into her Fox Run Apartment Complex, she drove over to the mailboxes to retrieve their mail. She pulled up to the maze of mailboxes and searched for hers like always. "I don't know why I always do this," she said to herself, bewildered by her lack of memory in finding something as small as a mailbox. But then again, she reasoned that they all look alike, so she didn't feel that bad after all. She grabbed the handful of mail and walked back to the car. She patted her stomach and said in a low voice, "Oh, baby, mommy is about to feed you breakfast in a little bit," as her stomach growled.

Lucy got back in the car and pulled away from the mailbox curb and drove to her building to park. She was shining brightly today, because her life was coming together where it seemed to have been falling apart before. Today, at the rate things were going, there just might be a chance that she'd be able to have this family she envisioned all the time.

She also was happy about what the doctor had told her about the baby. He said that she was a little further along than the projected five months already assumed. He said she was closer to six. The baby was growing regularly, developing well, and it was a boy. Her due date was only 90 to 100 days away, and to top it all off, Pretty E had her on an emotional high. *Fuck it, I'm wasted!* she thought, and turned the key in the door.

■■■■■■

Pretty E was sitting up in bed watching ESPN Sports Center's *Not So Top Ten Plays of the Week*, when heard Lucy come into the apartment. "Damn, she's back from her doctor's appointment already?" he asked himself, remembering it wasn't that long ago that she had gotten out of bed.

Lucy had been spoiling him like crazy for the past week or two, doing everything from cooking to bathing him, sucking and fucking him, all the way down to pampering him and doctoring him back to health. He looked down at his burns and was pleased at how well they were healing. The doctor said that Lucy was doing a spectacular job at tending to his burns. She did exactly what the doctor advised her to do, from scraping the scabs, the part that Pretty E hated, to washing the burns thoroughly with a burn medication soap. Lucy had become more than just a fuck to him. She had become his friend, not to mention the mother of his child, something he had to remind himself of all the time, because he still couldn't believe he was going to be a daddy.

"Hi, baby. Did you eat yet?" Lucy asked him when she walked into the bedroom and saw him sitting up watching television.

"Nah, not yet."

"Are you hungry?"

"A little bit," he answered.

"Alright, let me sit down for a little while first," she said, and kicked off her shoes before coming over to sit. "Baby, guess what?"

"What?"

"The doctor said we're having a boy. Ain't that just fabulous!"

"Yes, that's just stunning!" Pretty E teased her in his own little white boy interpretation.

"Shut up!" she said, and poked her lips out. "It's not my fault I talk like that."

"Damn, baby, relax! I'm only teasing."

"Oh?" she said, and looked at his burns. "Baby, your scars are healing up well. The doctor said you can get your skin grafted when they completely heal up, but you might not need a skin graft because they're healing so well," she said, rubbing her fingers across some of the healed spots. "What do you want to eat?" she asked.

"Some waffles, eggs, and sausage," he answered.

"Alright, let me get up then. I'll be right back," she said, and left the room.

Pretty E looked on as she switched her way out of the room, and smiled. *Damn, my baby got a "phat" ass! I don't know what it is they putting in the food, but these white girls getting phat as a muthafucka!* he thought, remembering seeing a phat ass white girl nearly everywhere he looked. On T.V., in the mall, at the clubs, in the supermarket, at the hospital, they were everywhere, and he was sure glad to have his.

"I wonder how my boy is doing? I ain't talked to him in a couple of days now," he said to himself as he thought about Rasul. Tameeka's death had weighed heavy on him, but he was coming along. The burial was his lowest point, the thing that had depressed him the most, because they lowered his wife in the dirt. It wasn't a bad dream to him anymore, it was reality. She was gone. However, since the funeral two weeks ago, he had been up moving around, laughing, smiling and shit. It seemed like he was back to his old self.

Pretty E grabbed the house phone at his bed side and began dialing his number.

■■■■■■

Rasul was sitting on the same couch that Tameeka used to sit in, rocking baby Tameeka in his arms. "Hey Mom-Mom, that's your mommy right there," Rasul said as he looked up at his new picture of Tameeka.

He had a real artist paint a portrait of her the size of a billboard almost, and hung it up over the fireplace. She looked stunning too. It was a painted picture of her on their wedding day, standing in the backyard by the pond, with her hands on her stomach.

"And guess what? That's you that she's holding," he continued. The more he stared at the picture, the more it seemed like the picture was staring back. He missed Tameeka dearly, but the thing that kept him strong was the memories he had of her. Her smile, her attitude, and that sexy as walk stayed fresh in his mind. "Damn I miss you, baby!" he said aloud, as if she could hear him.

Then the phone rang. "Hello!"

"Wha's up, cousin? How you been? Why you ain't call a mu'fucka?"

"'Cause, man, y'all lives don't revolve around me. I know y'all have other shit to do than to cater to me all the time, feel me?" he replied.

"Yeah, I feel you, but we family, nigga. It's never a bad time or inconvenience for me, you know? I'll drop everything at the drop of a dime for you, nigga."

"I know dat's right, and I'll do the same for you, nigga."

"I know you will."

"So, wha's up? What chu doing?"

"Nothing. Sitting here with Lucy. You know she's having a little boy, right?"

"Say word?"

"Word!"

"Awwww shit! How is the world going to deal with another you?"

"Yeah nigga, how they gon' act?"

"Beats the hell out of me, cousin."

"How's li'l Meek-Meek doin'?"

"She's cool, sittin' here on my lap looking like her mom as usual."

"You ain't lying."

"You know what?" Rasul asked. "Sometimes I think she's Tameeka reincarnated, 'cause I'll be damn if she don't want me all to herself, just like her mom did."

"How's Jaquaan?"

"He's good. He's been up Philly for the past couple of days. Some young girl got 'im wide open. I think his young ass is pussy whipped! That's why his jumper fell off," he said, and they shared a laugh. "How's Tammy?"

"She's alright. She just wants me to come home, that's all. It's killing her to know that I'm down here with Lucy. She can't accept the fact that she's a white girl, and she's pregnant by me. If it was a sista, she probably wouldn't care. That's how crazy she is. I want to go home too, cousin, but that bitch threw that hot water on me. She's lucky I ain't kill her ass!"

"So, is that why you ain't going home?"

"Yeah, she's on punishment."

"You a lying ass! Nigga, you think Tammy is going to kill yo' ass!" he laughed.

"Oh, you got jokes, huh?"

"Nah, I'm bullshitin'. So, what's up? How you feel about Lucy?"

"I love Lucy. I love her *and* Tammy, but shit just ain't working out right. I want both of them. I know I ain't making any choice."

"You gotta do some 'em."

"I will. I'll think of some 'em," he said, and then continued. "Alright man, let me go. My baby just brought me my breakfast."

"I heard dat. Look, call me later on or some 'em," Rasul said, and hung up the phone. It hadn't even sat on the receiver for a hot second before it rang again and he was answering it. "Hello!"

"Hey, son, how's it going?" Frankie asked, and Rasul's heart dropped. This was the phone call he dreaded. There was no way in the world that he was going to be able to kill Lucy, not now anyway. Not after what he experienced a couple weeks ago. Loosing Tameeka made him see things totally different than before. She was his everything, and after the phone call he just had with Pretty E, he understood that Lucy was *his* everything too. Plus, she was having his baby.

Rasul had to think of something to tell Frankie now, because Lucy couldn't die. There was no way he wanted Pretty E to feel what he felt every day when he lost Tameeka, but if Lucy died, that's exactly what would happen. "It's going good! Wha's new with you?"

"Nothing much. Just having my balls busted every day by the Family about this Lucy broad. How are you doing? Are you okay to do the... you know?" he asked, but didn't specify what because they were on the phone.

"No, not really. I don't think it should be, you know, at all. She's pregnant, she apologized, and she means well. I've forgiven her."

"Are you feeling okay?"

"Yeah!"

"I mean, are you really feeling okay? Because you're talking like you lost your mind. Now I know you been through some shit, but if you can't go through with the... you know... I'll gladly handle it. There won't be any hard feelings about this either, because I understand your side. But she has to go. Talk to you later," he said and hung up.

What am I going to do? Rasul asked himself as he looked at the phone in his hand.

Chapter Seventeen

The sky was pitch black, but the stars shined brightly. Every constellation, from the Big Dipper, to Pegasus the horse, all the way down to Orion's Belt, glowed and stood out amongst the rest of the stars present tonight. The moon was full, and nothing felt out of place, which was odd, because normally a full moon sent off an eerie feeling.

Dog drove the car smoothly, while Pretty E lay back. They cruised the city from block to block, collecting their money form their foot soldiers. The 'caine at the warehouse was nearly gone. There wasn't anymore 'caine at the house on Vandever Avenue, and they were debating on whether to get anymore from Frankie when it was all gone.

The game was over for them in their book, but for some reason they couldn't let go. Why? They didn't know. The reason was because they were addicted. Everyone who came in contact with the game became addicted, because it gave you gratification for everything you did. The game gave you power if you were weak. The game gave you money if you were poor. The game gave you women if you were ugly, and the game gave you respect in more ways than one. How can anybody not become addicted to something as good as that? How can you not become addicted to having thousands of dollars in your pocket and hadn't had to work anywhere in the country? That's why it was so hard to leave the game alone, and that's why it was hard for Dog and Pretty E to make a decision.

"Yo, man," Dog began. "Ain't it fucked up what happened to Tameeka?"

"Damn right! That shit made me value my life a little more than I already did, feel-me? She was healthy as shit. That just goes to show you that tomorrow ain't promised."

"I feel that. So, what you goin' to do?"

"About what?"

"About the game, 'cause I'm where Rasul is at today. I'm tired of the hassle that comes along with the bullshit. We already got everything we need, so why keep going? Man, we got too much to lose. What? We got about 15 birds left, right?"

"Nah, we got two crates, so that's like 30," Pretty E told him.

"Alright then, here's what we should do. Let's give everything we got left to our lieutenants all at once. Fuck it! Give it to them in one big whop, and then we'd be done. Won't be no more work left, just one big cash pick-up. We don't owe Frankie no more money, so we can let them go to him for what he gave them to us for. Feel-me? Look out for them little niggaz, 'cause they sure looked out for us. Them niggaz made us millionaires."

"I'm wit' dat."

"Well, let's do this shit then," Dog said. "Call them li'l niggaz up, the ones we just left too, and let them niggaz know not to go anywhere, because we got some 'em for them," he said. "And tell them not to go nowhere, 'cause we goin' to be too dirty to ride around looking for 'em"

"Aw'ight," Pretty E responded, and began to dial numbers.

■■■■■■

Ricky and Nicky Stango received the call and order from Frankie early in the afternoon to perform the hit on Lucy. The call was what they had been waiting for, because it gave them a chance to do what they loved to do, and that was killing. Just watching a person scream, beg, kick, and crawl for their life gave them a feeling of power that had an equal to none. They didn't have an ounce of remorse or love in their hearts for anyone or anybody but Frankie and their families. The Capelli Family and their own were old school *La Cosa Nostra* to the core.

Their job tonight was no different in their eyes than the other 100 or more they had already done over the years. The only thing that made this one different to them in a sense was that they yearned for this particular hit, because it was Lucy. It was more than a job to them, it was personal. She was the pig, snitch, and rat who had worked undercover for the Feds and got their brother, Lenny (Fat Boy) Ionni, seventeen years in the can.

Ricky drove the black Lincoln Continental down Route 40, and as usual, "Old Blue Eyes" Frank Sinatra played just a little above a whisper. It was a ritual for them to play Old Blue Eyes before every hit they'd done, because it set the tone for them. Frank's lyrics had a way of putting them in a mood for killing, and as the words to "My Way" oozed out the speakers, and that's how they felt all the time. They did things their way.

Ricky turned into the apartment complex and drove around until he found Building B. He pulled in a parking space next to a huge green trash Dumpster and parked the car.

Nicky, who was in the passenger seat, reached in the back seat for his little black "doctor's bag", the one he carried on every hit, and checked its contents. "All here," he said to himself, but loud enough for Ricky to hear him as he rummaged through the bag. The scalpel, knives, scissors, rags, and alcohol were all in place.

Ricky looked at his twin brother and shook his head, because he knew that his brother didn't have it all upstairs. He was a little mentally disturbed at times, and fluctuated back and forth into these little alter ego types of mind states. One minute he was like a mad scientist, and the next he was and evil doctor. *Today he must be the doctor,* Ricky thought.

Nicky zipped the bag up and said, "Come on, let's go," and he and his brother headed over to the apartment building.

■■■■■■

Rasul carried little Tameeka into her nursery, the one he had an interior decorator come and create, and lay her in the crib.

The entire room had been painted pink and white, with cartoon characters painted everywhere. Whinney the Pooh was on one wall, Snow White and the Seven Dwarfs were on another, while Cinderella, Mickey Mouse, and the entire Walt Disney World family was on the other. He also had the room miked for sound and connected to speakers that were placed throughout the house. He had this done so that no matter where he or Jaquaan were in the house, they would hear her whenever she would start crying.

He tucked her in until he was pleased with how cozy she looked, and then kissed her lightly on the cheek.

When he left out of her bedroom, he walked down the hallway into the master bedroom and stepped out on the balcony. He sat down at the table and stared out into space as he relaxed in the chair. The balcony had become his favorite place for quiet time, because this was where he shared some of his most intimate memories of Tameeka: Memories of him and her sitting out here eating dinner under a moonlit sky as soft music played from a from the bedroom. Memories of them sharing their dreams with one another while El Debarge crooned the lyrics to his song, "Dreams, A Simple Fantasy That I Wish Was Reality". Memories of her elbows on the table, resting her chin in her palms as she stared into his eyes while he tried to sing along. And memories of when his life was good when Meek-Meek was still around.

Rasul felt the tear drip off of his chin and land in his lap as memories of Tameeka flashed into his head like they so often did. Some of the images were so life-like that he could actually hear her voice.

"Damn!" he spoke out loud as he rose up from the chair he was sitting in. "I can't let my boy feel like this. I gotta tell 'im. I can't let Lucy go out like this."

Rasul grabbed the phone and began dialing Pretty E's number against everything he knew was wrong. Lucy's dying was business, but it was personal for his boy. "Fuck what Frankie talking about! Pretty E is my brother, just like Lenny (Fat Boy) Ionni is his, and it ain't going down like that," he said to himself as the phone started ringing. He looked over at the clock and saw that it read 10:45 p.m. and hoped that he didn't wait too late to move.

"Hello!" Pretty E answered.

"Yo, where you at?"

"I'm out and about. Why, wha's wrong?"

"Where's Lucy at?" he asked impatiently.

"Home. Why?"

"Damn!"

"Wha's wrong?"

"Yo, I just got a call from Frankie," he lied "He said he's sending Ricky and Nicky to kill Lucy."

"What! Kill Lucy for what?"

"For the shit she did before she disappeared. The shit dat got Lenny all that time."

"Man, she ain't no cop no more!"

"Once a cop, always a cop, that's how those Mob cats think. Yo, we ain't got that much time. Call Lucy and tell her not to answer the door, and meet me at the crib. Yo, where's Dog at?"

"He's wit' me!"

"Good! Look, let's get there, nigga, before it's too late," Rasul said, relieved that he told him, but prayed it wasn't too late. *I should have been told him,* he thought, and knew that he wouldn't be able to forgive himself if they didn't get there in time.

■■■■■■

Lucy stepped out of the tub after taking a long hot shower, and stood before the mirror. She poked at her cheeks with her fingers and said, "My God! I'm like, really like, getting huge!" as she noticed the chubbiness of her face. She looked down at her stomach and saw a lump appear on the side of it, then watched it disappear as fast as it appeared, then returned again. She lightly lay her hand on it and pressed, feeling the baby, move again. "I wonder if that was his feet," she asked herself.

Then she heard a knock on the door. "Where are his keys? I hope he didn't forget them somewhere again," she said to herself, and stepped into her thong underwear. She grabbed her robe from the bathroom door hook and slipped in it as she headed for the door.

"Knock! Knock! Knock!" the door sounded again.

"Okay, already!" she shouted." Here I come! You shouldn't have lost your keys again, Eric. You have to at least give me a chance to get there. I was in the shower," she explained as she fumbled with the locks. Just when she got to the last lock, her phone rang. *They'll call back later,* she told herself, and pulled the door open.

Chapter Eighteen

As cautious as Lucy was about every move she made in her life, she allowed herself to be caught off guard by the intruders, and it was the worst mistake of her life. She knew her life was over. There was no way in the world that she could be any kind of match to the huge man that stood before her. She tried to slam the door back shut, but he put his arm through the crack and powered it back open. He raised his hand and back slapped her across the jaw so hard that it literally knocked her out. She could tell by the way it popped that it was broken when she fell to the floor.

Lying on her back, she sat up and scooted across the floor on her butt as Ricky Stango stalked her down. "Please don't hurt me! I'm having a baby! Please!" she cried, trying to persuade them, but she knew they weren't robbers. Their faces looked too familiar, like she knew them from somewhere. *Who are they? Where do I know them from?* she asked herself as she looked for something to defend herself with. "Oh my God!" Terror signals went off in her head as she remembered who they were. They were Ricky and Nicky Stango, the Mob's hit men! They had allegedly been responsible for more than one hundred murders over the past twenty years, according to her memory of her police files of the Capelli Family, but they never were charged due to lack of evidence.

Ricky smiled as she squirmed away from him. He reached down and grabbed her by the hair and dragged her to her feet. With his free hand, he wrapped it around her throat and slammed her against the wall. "You fuckin' pig!" he said, and lifted her off her feet as her toes dangled, trying to find the carpet. *"Smack!"* his hand sounded as the free hand crashed against her already broken jaw, while Nicky neatly unpacked his doctor's bag on the living room coffee table.

Ricky saw her face turning blue and stared at her in the eyes. He watched intensely as the life slowly escaped her body, because that's what gave him his rush. He loved these types of moments so much, that it actually gave him an erection. "That's right, bitch! Die slowly. You'll never tell on another *La Cosa Nostra* now, will you?" he talked to her as she coughed her last breath of life, and her body went limp.

"Hey, Ricky, bring her over to the couch, will ya?" Nicky instructed, and Ricky threw her over his shoulder like a sack of potatoes.

Ricky lay her down on the couch, and for the next ten minutes, he cut, sliced, and pulled layers of her skin back. When he was finished with his makeshift operation on Lucy, the sight of what he had done to her would be branded on Pretty E's brain for the rest of his life.

He zipped up his doctor's bag, and they disappeared out of the door with another job well done, and their one hundred and first body.

■■■■■■

The race against time was useless, because she was gone. The phone call to Pretty E was a moment too late. When they arrived at the apartment, the sight of what they had done to Lucy would fill the three of them with blind fury. With a hatred that ran into the very marrow of their bones, the only thing that would even come close to the equivalence to what they had done would be the deaths of the men responsible for this heinous act.

Rasul was turning into the complex almost at the exact same time as Pretty E and Dog. They were moving so fast that he tapped his brakes and let him turn in first. They raced bumper to bumper through the complex, jumping speed bumps as if they weren't even there, and parked in front of the building.

Pretty E didn't even turn his car off before he jumped out and raced up the stairs to his apartment.

"Yo, wha's up?" Rasul asked, and Pretty E looked back over his shoulder and said, "She ain't answering the phone."

Rasul's heart dropped into his stomach. He hoped to God on everything he loved that what he thought hadn't come true, but there was this feeling that said it had.

He and Dog ran behind Pretty E and stood behind him at the door as he fumbled with the keys in the locks on the door. When he finally managed to open the door, they stepped into the apartment.

The sight of Lucy lying there lifeless was unbearable. She was on her back, drenched in a pool of blood on the couch. Her once white night robe had been dyed a dark crimson, as her thick blood soaked into the cushions on the couch. The murder had been committed in such a careless and messy way, that blood was splattered everywhere; on the walls, the carpet, and the window blinds. It looked like they just tore her apart, and with every tear, her blood shot out of her like juice from a ripe piece of fruit.

The most sickening and disturbing part about the whole act was that the baby she was carrying had been cut from her belly and placed in her arms. The lifeless little body looked helpless as it clutched on to its mother and jerked from the nerve endings that were still alive.

Pretty E dropped to his knee's and cried his heart out as he looked at the person he had come to love, and his child laying murdered before his eyes. He looked up to Dog and Rasul blankly, searching them for comfort in anyway he could, but there was nothing they could do to help. The sight of what happened to Lucy and the baby had them fucked up too. The only thing left for them to do was to channel everything they felt inside right now into rage and fuel for revenge, and that's exactly what they did.

They didn't have to say one word as they looked into one another's eyes, because their heart of hearts said it all. They were going to war. The Capelli Family had crossed the line.

■■■■■■

Detective Cohen was sitting in his office trying to piece together any and every piece of evidence he could find to tie together and build a case against Rasul, Dog, and Pretty E. He was determined to land them in jail for the murder of his partner, Detective Armstrong, and the murders of the missing persons, Shelly and Brian (Bo-Bo), who disappeared years ago.

Working on his fourth cup of black coffee, no sugar or creamer, he was amped from all the caffeine. His working hours had long passed by, but he had become accustomed to staying overtime even though he wasn't on the clock. He stayed, because landing them in jail where he knew they belonged was a must.

Frustrated, Cohen slammed his folder shut on his desk and stood to leave his office and head for the door when his phone rang. "Hello, Cohen speaking," he answered.

"Hello, Detective Cohen. This is Lieutenant Allen of Homicide. We met over a couple of years ago at your partner's funeral."

"Oh yeah, I remember. How's it going?"

"I think we've just came across a body that may be of some importance to you. I know we're from different jurisdictions, me being a New Castle County officer and you being a Wilmington officer, but we're still on the same team. I know how important you partner's murder was to you, and I know how bad you want to solve it, so when I saw the body I had to call you first. Her name is Jennifer Vault, ex-federal agent. Beautiful woman. It's a shame the way she was dismantled."

"Are you serious?"

"Yeah, it's a shame too."

"Where are you now?"

"We're in Fox Run Apartments or Town House— whatever you want to call it—out here on Route 40. I called you first, because when the Feds get wind of what happened in the next twenty minutes, they'll be here. You got like a half hour head start, so I advise you to get here now," Allen finished.

"Thanks. I'm on my way."

Cohen couldn't believe what he just heard. Federal Agent Vault, the officer who turned lawyer and just won the biggest case in State's recent history was found dead. "I know they're connected in some kind of way, or they will be. I know it!" he told himself, talking about Rasul, Pretty E, and Dog. He knew from experience that this was in no way finished, not by a long shot.

Detective Cohen snatched his keys from his pants pocket and trotted across the parking lot towards his unmarked Caprice. He threw his light up on the dashboard, revved the engine, and slammed it into gear. The tires squealed when he took off, leaving skid marks in the parking lot as he headed towards Route 40 to the murder scene.

He searched his mind for anything that might make sense of this murder, but that would take a minute, because Lucy was connected to too may people. What he had to do was start with everybody he knew that was connected to her, then start the process of elimination. He knew that the Feds weren't responsible, and he also knew that Pretty E couldn't be the murderer either, because that wouldn't make sense. Everyone knew that he and Jennifer were together as a couple and about to be the parents of a child, so he was out. Besides, she had just won a trial for them that would have sure gotten them twenty or more years had they lost.

Then there was the Capelli Family. She had done the unthinkable to them. She had managed to infiltrate their shield of protection and get inside of their secret lives in order to land one of the most prominent figures they had in the organization in jail for the next seventeen years.

Lastly, there was Tammy Brown, Pretty E's girlfriend. He didn't think that she could be responsible for an act like this, but when he got there and saw the scene, Tammy Brown had become his lead suspect. It was hard for him to believe that she could do something like this at first—her or anybody else for that matter. But when a women is scorned, you could never tell. They were capable of anything. And right now, it looked like a clean-cut case of the jealous girlfriend. However, the baby being torn from the mother like that was a whole different story. Then, again, here recently there have been several cases of this same act reported across the United States. *Maybe she was a copy cat,* he thought, but he needed answers... *now!*

Chapter Nineteen

Pretty E had gotten about all of twenty minutes sleep last night before being snatched back into reality. Sleep was a way of escaping problems or avoiding them from time to time, but his mind wouldn't allow him to sleep. There was too much going on in his mind for him to rest, and even when he did start to relax, it would happen again. Images of Lucy lying in a pool of blood on the couch would pop into his head. He cried. His heart ached for her presence. His mind wondered *why?* He asked himself why he wasn't there. His nose would tingle, his eyes would water, and he was crying again.

Today though, at the house on Vandever Avenue, he would plan his revenge—their revenge, his, Lucy's and their unborn child's revenge. He called Dog and Rasul to make sure they were on point and had handled what he asked them to do, which was stupid, because he knew they would. They had already.

When he arrived at the house, he noticed that Dog and Rasul's cars were already there. He parked behind Dog's and got out to head up the busted sidewalk to the front door. Before he could use his key in the door, Dog was already pulling it open.

"Wha's good, cousin? You aw'ight, nigga?" Dog asked, seeing clearly by the bags under his eyes that he wasn't.

"Nah, man. I ain't aw'ight, but I will be…" he paused before saying, "As soon as I get these niggaz's heads resting forever," he finished.

"Don't worry about dat, cousin. We are definitely going to handle that." "Where's Rasul at?" he asked, looking around the house.

"He upstairs. I think he's in the bathroom."

Rasul heard the door open when his boy came in, but he was upstairs in the bathroom. He didn't have to use it; he just needed a place to think. He sat on the edge of the bathtub smoking a cigarette, while he thought about what happened. He couldn't believe Frankie would still go through with the hit, especially after what he just went through by losing Tameeka. *He could have at least waited until she had the baby,* he thought as he blew smoke from his nose. *I guess that muthafucka really don't give a fuck about me after all,* he concluded.

This was the second time Frankie had done some shit to Rasul's disapproval. The first time was when after they talked and Rasul asked that he'd be given a chance to talk to Hit-Man before Frankie sent Ricky and Nicky, Frankie sent them anyway. Now this. And as he thought, he thought of the phrase, "Business, never personal." He realized that Frankie wouldn't hesitate to put a bullet in his head. Now, as he came to the conclusion of what he had to do, he understood that this was "business," but it was also "personal!"

Rasul joined his boys, Pretty E and Dog downstairs in the living room, and understood what friendship was all about. He really loved these two niggaz to death and would walk through hell with them. He entered the room to take a seat on the floor.

It pained his heart to the very core to see his boy Pretty E pace the floor like he was pacing it. The pain he felt inside was unimaginable. It was the kind of pain you couldn't take medicine for. The kind of wound you couldn't put a band-aid on. The kind of hurt that wouldn't allow you to sleep, eat, or think of anything else but vengeance, and Rasul new all about it. He experienced everything Pretty E was going through right now, the night that he lost Tameeka. Only for him, there was no one to take vengeance out on. It was different this time, because they had culprits, who are the Capelli Family.

Pretty E, Dog, and Rasul had all come to the conclusion that the best way to hit the Capelli Family was to hit them at Li'l Italy, the bar and lounge. They had pondered over a multitude of ways to get even, but none was sweeter than this way. If they followed everything exactly the way they planned it, the job would be flawless. They would be able to hit almost, if not all of the Capelli Family at one time. The time they would do it was next week during the Monday night football game. They knew from previous Monday nights they attended that all the major players in the Capelli Family would be there.

Pietro (The Hard Headed One) Capone would be there.

Augustino (The Bomber) Giovanni would be there. He earned the name "Bomber" because he played with C-4 like a child played with Silly Putty.

Frank Damone (Nero) Fraganelli would be there. He earned the name "Nero" because of his dark skinned complexion. As a child growing up in Sicily, he was teased about his complexion. The name Nero in Italian means nigger or Negro, so it offended him. Then, as he grew older, he learned to except the name because it was who he was. He learned through school that hundreds of years ago, there was an African king named Hannibal who conquered Sicily on elephants, and fathered many, many children. That was the reason he was so dark complexioned. It also was the reason why so many Italians disliked black people, because black was who they were, they just were in a lighter skin. History proves this fact.

Joey (The Fox) Vito, Ricky and Nicky Stango, and Frankie would also be there.

The way they planned it, they were all sitting ducks.

Rasul and Dog called every lieutenant they had on every side of town, and told them it was urgent that they meet them at the house on Vandever Avenue. The Urgency and sternness in their voices when they gave the order didn't need an explanation at to why. It just said, "Come on!" So when Rasul, Dog, and Pretty E heard the door, they already knew who was on the other side. It was their crew, a posse full of crazy young boys who didn't fear anything.

The first ones to walk in were E-Money Bags and Streetz from the Hill-Top. They were the wildest of all the lieutenants, and it showed as they came in the house.

"Wha's good?" Money Bags asked, blunt dangling from his lips and an ashy green Remy Martin bottle in his back pocket.

"Yeah, niggaz, wha's good?" added Streetz, eyes half shut from chewing Percocets and downing Remy as he stood on his Timberland laces with his pants sagging. The gun he held tucked in his waistband was obvious to the eye because of its huge handle. Rasul knew it was a .45 cal.

Bobby Dimes and Jewelz came in next. They were from the east side of town, and the pretty boys out of the lieutenants. They took after Pretty E, but don't confuse them as anything other then deadly. Their pretty boy demeanors had nothing in common with their lifestyles. They were dangerous, and the calluses on their trigger fingers proved it.

Shay-Ball, Monk, and Boop were from the projects in Riverside. That's all the needs to be said about them. They were handpicked by Hit-Man himself, and he never picked anyone, so these three had to be special, and Rasul knew why too. They were stone killers, and had accounted for most of the bodies around when they first started, staking their claim when he came home from prison.

Mar and Shizz from Market Street came in next, followed by K.B. and Ghetto from New Castle.

Lastly came Damon and Mark, Rasul's prodigies. He handpicked Damon himself, because from day one he knew Damon was a money getter, and it was proven to be right. Out of all the lieutenants, Damon was the paid one. He was a mogul when it came to being an entrepreneur and stacking money. Since they started doing business together, Rasul watched as him and Mark opened up store after store, car lots, and soul food restaurants. The boys were doing it, and Rasul loved it. The thing he loved the most was that they still were street-ready. Money hadn't made them soft, and it showed because they were here.

For the next twenty minutes or so, Rasul, Dog, and Pretty E explained the plan from top to bottom and side to side, until they were sure everyone was on the same page. They were there the moment they found out what happened to Pretty E's girl and baby.

So it was set. They were to meet here at Vandever Avenue next Monday at 7:00 p.m. on the dot. The destination: Li'l Italy.

■■■■■■

Li'l Italy on Monday nights was the liveliest bar, lounge, and social club in Wilmington for wise guys and made men in the Mob. To a person new to a scene of this magnitude, or to someone on the outside looking in, Li'l Italy would probably look like a scene cut straight from the movie, "Goodfellas". The entire look of the club, from the "wise guys" posted up in little groups flooding the bar, to the "made men" holding down the tables and booths with their girlfriends, Li'l Italy had organized crime written all over it.

Monday nights to the Capelli Family were their favorite, because it was a time for them to escape the stress of the wife and kids, and a time for them to relax and spend some quality time with their mistress. It was a time they told their wives they spent gambling and drinking with the fellas, but the wives knew that was a lie. They new Monday nights were really spent with the home-wrecking bitches, the ones the wives chose to call in their heavy Italian accents, "Fuckin' sluts!"

■■■■■■

Joey's wife Angela, the head of the "non-existent" wives group she started but never made official, would always bring light to situations such as these. She was the animated one, the one who spoke out for them all, the one who talked back to Joey and gave them all strength to talk back to their own husbands. She was the one who said what they were all thinking but were afraid to say. She was the one, who at their own little gatherings on Monday nights, was called upon to save the day, and like always, she came through.

"You know what?" she began. "There's no real reason for us to be sad or upset. In fact, we should be happy. Let the fuckin' sluts have the out of shape ass-holes. They've been with our husbands for years. Now they can do all of the dirty work. Our days of sucking peter and taking it up the ass are over! The fuckin' sluts can do that shit, while we cash checks, spend money, raise the children, and fuck missionary style every now and then," she finished, and they all enjoyed a laugh as they sat around and applied way too much makeup to each others faces. Angela's words made them feel good. They always did, but they still were curious about the club. That was something they'd never get to find out.

■■■■■

Back inside the social club, the huge wide screen televisions were all fixed on ABC for the Monday night game between the Eagles and the Giants. It was an NFC East rivalry that was sure to be a good one, especially since the Giants activated newly acquired Plaxico Burress, a 6'5 wide out that made a huge target for Eli Manning.

While John Madden and Frank Gifford talked football, Frankie walked around with a pen and a note pad, jotting down all the bets that were being placed so there wouldn't be any dumb shit at the end of the night. After he finished doing that, he sat back and looked over the club and felt good. He felt good because there were no more bad bones out on the Capelli Family. Their slate had been wiped clean again the night Ricky and Nicky took out Lucy, the ex-federal agent whose investigation landed a real good man behind bars; Lenny (Fat Boy) Ionni.

Frankie walked towards the back of the club and disappeared behind the door marked "Private". He sat in his swivel chair behind the desk and opened the drawer. He gabbed one of the many prescription pill bottles that were in there and popped one of the small pellets into his mouth and felt it dissolve on his tongue. Almost instantly he felt the effects of the nitroglycerin take control over his irregular heartbeat, and then wondered about his other illness. He wondered if it was true about the way people said cancer ate at your body. If so, Frankie sure didn't want to die that way. He'd rather be taken out by a bullet or a car accident than by a slow and suffering death. If he could have read the future though, he would have felt a whole lot better, because suffering was something he would not do.

■■■■■

Pretty E, Dog, and Rasul put the last crate of bottled cocktails in the trunk of the squatter they brought just for tonight's hit, and then went into the house. The clock on the wall in the living room was the only thing left in the house on Vandever Avenue, but it was of great importance right now. It was the only thing that the three of them had to keep track of the time with, and everything they had planned to do for tonight had to be done on time for it to work the way they planned it.

Only a half hour left, Pretty E thought, and the longest week of his life would be over. He knew deep down in his heart of hearts that the only way he'd be able to get over seeing Lucy and his unborn child lying there in that pool of blood would be to get revenge on the people responsible for it, and the time finally had come.

Rasul was ready for war too, but there was something inside of him that made him feel uneasy. Yes, revenge was a must, but why did it have to come at the cost of him and Frankie's relationship? That's what was making him feel uneasy. It was the love they had for one another that would come to an end that was bothering him the most. *Damn! Why does it have to end this way?* he asked himself, then remembered something Frankie had told him a long time ago, a time they shared together in the confines of the walls behind the McKean Federal Prison:

"Rasul," Frankie had said. "The game ain't fair!"

And now, for the first time Rasul understood what he meant when he said that. "Damn, Frankie, you don't know how right you were," Rasul said to himself, and looked up at the clock. Ten minutes.

Dog didn't really care one way or another about what happened tonight, except that they all made it back in one piece and got the revenge all at the same time. He did have this thought; that this would be the last time he'd ever ride like this again for his boys or anyone else. It was about his wife and kids now. Rasul's words had finally penetrated and sunk into his thick skull, because his days in the game were over, just as sure as they were for Rasul. The game and the life they lived had cost both of his friends someone dear to them. For Pretty E, he lost Lucy violently, the same way they had been so violent with other people. For Rasul, he lost Tameeka in a totally different manner, but it probably happened for something they did in the past. That's another reason Dog wanted out, because he was a firm believer in good and bad karma, and for some reason it bypassed him. He did, however, lose someone close to him when he lost Hit-Man, but he didn't lose a wife or child like they had, so just that in itself was a blessing. That's why he knew that after tonight he was going to count his blessings and move on with his life.

"Yo!" Dog called for their attention. "Y'all alright?"

"Yeah, I'm cool," Rasul said.

"Yeah, I'm cool too," Pretty E said, then asked, "Why you say dat?"

"'Cause we just sitting here not saying nothing," Dog answered.

"Yeah, that's 'cause a nigga in thought," Rasul said. "I'm just ready to get this shit over with and move on. Start growing in these business moves and shit. Expanding out, feel me?"

"Dat's where I'm at too, man," Dog coat-tailed.

"Yeah, me too," Pretty E agreed.

"Yo man, in case I don't get to tell you two niggaz later on, I'ma tell you now. Yo, on everything I love, I love you two niggaz, hear?" Dog said seriously.

"Man, go ahead with that bullshit, nigga! We going to be alright," Rasul said.

"Yeah, we might be, but nigga, we about to go to war with the Mob," Dog reminded them.

"Yeah, nigga, that's true, but we got a Mob of crazy young niggaz too! Fuck da Mob, nigga! *We* da Mob!" Pretty E reminded him.

Then there was a knock on the door. They looked up at the clock, and it was seven o'clock on the dot. The posse was accounted for.

"I told you, nigga, we da Mob," Pretty E said and smiled. "Now, let's go handle this shit!"

"I hear dat!" Dog said, and Rasul smiled.

"I love you two Niggaz!" Rasul said, and they stepped out of the house and into the presence of their thirteen crazy young boyz, ready for war.

■■■■■■

At the half, the score was 17-10 New York, and Frankie was more than pleased. He had bet nearly twenty thousand dollars on the New York Giants, taking them with the six points they'd been given, so in reality, the score was really 23-10.

Frankie walked over to his under-boss, Joey Vito, and asked him had he heard from or spoken to Rasul. Joey replied that he hadn't since Lucy's death.

Frankie began to wonder why he hadn't heard from him in over a week, and couldn't come up with anything other than he must still be grieving over the death of Tameeka, which was understandable, but he still could have called. Never in a million years would he have believed that his reason for not calling was because of Lucy's death, because he knew it had to happen. In fact, Rasul was supposed to do it.

What Frankie didn't understand or failed to look at was that the death of Tameeka hurt Rasul dearly. It was a pain unreal. A pain he wouldn't have wished on his worse enemy, so when it happened to Lucy and he saw the pain it gave Pretty E, it filled him with rage. Rage, because he sympathized with Pretty E. He knew what he felt, so when it happened to Pretty E, he felt that it happened to him all over again.

"How could Frankie do something like that to her, knowing that she was pregnant with Pretty E's child?" was the question Rasul asked himself over and over again, but could not come up with any reasonable answers. Revenge was the only way to get even.

Frankie was totally unaware of the way Rasul was feeling about what had happened. There were no warning signs, or anything foul that even gave suspicion to Frankie that his bond had been broken, and that maybe he should be on guard. For the first time in his entire life, Frankie had let his emotions override his intelligence. An absence of anyone should have sent off a warning sign, but it was Rasul. It was his adopted son, the one whom he loved like his own.

"He just needs some space, that's all," Frankie decided, not realizing he was putting himself in check in the chess game of life. One more mistake was checkmate, game over.

"The game ain't fair!"

■■■■■■

The plan was to ambush the social club unexpectedly, that's why they chose tonight. They knew Frankie and the Capelli Family's entire operation from front to back. They knew everything, from how it ran, to the inside shit. They knew shit even the members didn't know because of Frankie. Frankie told Rasul everything—his biggest mistake—but he wanted him to know. He wanted Rasul to be able to run his operation the same way he did, and that's why Rasul, Dog, and Pretty E were so successful. The reality was that they too were a Mob, just a Black one, a Black organized crime family with no name.

Rasul, Dog, and Pretty E knew Li'l Italy inside out. They knew there were only two ways in and out of the bar and lounge, and that was through the front and back doors. There was a huge stained glass window at the entrance of the club right next to the front door that read "Li'l Italy's Bar & Lounge" in fancy writing, and a few small ones. That's why they had the "cocktails", two crates full of them, totaling twenty-eight bottles filled with gasoline and a rag stuck in the top of them. They figured that once they tossed them through the windows, everyone inside of the club would stampede out of both exits, and they'd be there to pluck them off as they came out.

"Shoot everything that's moving!" was the briefing that Rasul, Dog, and Pretty E gave Baby Dimes, Jewelz, Boop, Monk, Shay-Ball, and the rest of them, and they loved it. They couldn't wait to take the Mob to war. This would be the most talked about event since 9/11 in the country, and they'd probably make history as being the first Black Mob take on *La Cosa Nostra* since the late great Bumpy Johnson did it in the Harlem renaissance days.

The only thing was, they wanted to win and get away with it. If they followed each and every rule step by step, and executed them the way they were drawn out, they would get away with it, *and* make history. They knew that if they completed an act like this, each and every one of them would be placed in a ranking so high that they'd be praised by the underworld, and that meant power.

Four cars deep, with Rasul, Dog, and Pretty E leading the way, their lieutenants followed them across the city limits until they reached the Italian section of the city. They parked the cars four blocks away in every direction, with no two cars near each other, and walked to the corner of 7th and Scott Street. The street was empty, which was a good thing, as they all looked across the street at the bar and lounge called Li'l Italy, sitting on the corner.

"Look, after we do this shit," Rasul began, "No running away from the scene. It draws attention. Stay calm, walk back to your cars and park them where I told y'all to and go home. The two trucks will pick up every car and take them to New Jersey where they will be crushed at the junk yard, so don't worry about fingerprints and shit. Just get home. I'll meet with each and every one of you tomorrow, so relax, okay?" he finished, and there was just a nod of heads.

Bobby Dimes, Jewelz, Boop, Monk and Shay-Ball stationed themselves at the back door with their guns drawn. Rasul, Dog, Pretty E, Damon, and Mark played the front, while Shizz, Mar, K.B. and Ghetto positioned themselves in the front and on the sides by the windows with the cocktails. As soon as Rasul gave them the nod, they lit the rags and began tossing them into the windows.

When the first cocktail came crashing through the window in the front it didn't bust. It just rolled across the floor with the rag burning.

Ricky Stango, the keenest of them all, jumped up from the table he was sitting at with his girlfriend and picked it up off the floor. He ran across Li'l Italy's makeshift dance floor and threw it out of the same window it came crashing through, and watched as it exploded outside on the pavement. When the flames burst in the sky it gave off just enough light for Ricky to see that the club was surrounded by Rasul and his crew. He knew it was them, because he and Pretty E made eye contact with each other.

Ricky looked back over his shoulder at everyone who was wondering what was going on and said, "Get the ladies out of here, 'cause we're under attack!"

"Attack?" Frankie asked, making sure he heard the words right.

"Yeah, attack!" Ricky assured him. "And by those fuckin' moolies!" he finished, and Frankie lowered his head in shame.

Cocktails were coming through everywhere now, only this time they were exploding. The Capelli Family had been caught completely off guard. People were screaming at the top of their lungs as the building burned, along with the clothes on their backs as they tried to get out of Li'l Italy. The ones who did manage to get out were greeted by gunshots and bullets they never saw coming. The Bomber took one right between the eyes, as did the Hard Headed One, but the rest of them perished. The entire Capelli Family had been wiped out tonight, and all in a matter of moments.

Frankie, Joey (The Fox) Vito, and Ricky and Nicky Stango were the last ones left. They stood behind the door marked "Private" and nervously armed themselves with guns as they listened to the massacre that was taking place beyond the doors. They heard the screams, listened to the shots, and tried to imagine how bad the fire had grown, because now they heard shit collapsing onto tables and the floors.

"We have to get up out of here now!" Joey exclaimed, fear evident in his voice.

"Yeah, we do. Come on, Frankie," Nicky said, grabbing hold of his arm.

"Here I come. Just let me take these," he said, and popped two more nitroglycerin pills to calm his heart. But they didn't work this time. This time was real. It was his fear that pushed his heart this time, and the reality of not knowing what lay beyond the door for them.

Frankie followed Nicky, Ricky, and Joey out into the hallway towards the back door. With all that was happening so fast, it seemed as if they'd been in that room for hours, but it had only been about four to five minutes. In just that little bit of time, the fire damage had claimed nearly the whole Capelli Family, and it saddened Frankie's heart, because he knew he had slipped. All he could see through the smoke and flames were lifeless bodies on fire sprawled all over the place, and the smell of the burnt flesh turned his stomach.

When Ricky and Nicky reached the back door, they stepped out with their guns blazing. The shots caught Bobby Dimes and Boop by surprise, because they thought it was over. The bullets from both guns caught each of them high in the torso, but the damage wasn't life threatening. The impact just threw them to the ground. Ricky and Nicky were about to finish them off but were caught with a barrage of bullets from Jewelz, Monk and Shay-Ball that left them lying where they stood.

Frankie and Joey were frozen stiff.

Rasul, Dog, and Pretty E told the half of the crew that were in the front of the building with them to go ahead and leave, which they did, but only after Damon had to be begged by Rasul to do so. That's why Rasul loved him, because Damon was just like him, but wiser than he was at that age. After seeing them off, they made their way towards the back to see what was going on with all the gunshots. When they got back there, they saw Boop and Bobby Dimes lying on the sidewalk being hovered over by Jewelz, Monk and Shay-Ball.

"Yo, get them up out of here! It's a wrap! All them muthafuckas are dead," Rasul said, feeling good about the revenge.

Then something told him to look towards the back door. When he did, he saw Ricky and Nicky laid out, but that wasn't it. It was the sight of seeing Frankie and Joey (The Fox) Vito standing there frozen stiff that aroused and deflated him all at the same time. Rasul stood to his feet after checking on Boop and Bobby Dimes, and again told them to leave. With his gun out, he walked towards Frankie and Joey as the rest of his posse left, all except for Dog and Pretty E.

"Hurry up, man! Just bust them two muthafuckas and come on!" Dog said, hearing sirens off in a distance.

"Alright man, hold up!" Rasul said, as Dog followed him to the back door.

"Hurry up, y'all! I got it out here!" Pretty E said from the sidewalk as they disappeared behind the little brick cubical that was built behind the club. The cubical was like a little patio or something, but it was blocked off from the street. No one could see beyond the walls of it unless they poked their head around its entrance.

Rasul walked straight up to Joey and put the barrel of his .40 cal. straight to his forehead and pulled the trigger, blowing his brains out, along with his toupee, up against a portion of the wall. Then he turned to Frankie and looked at him with tears in his eyes. "Frankie, can I let you live?" he asked, and meant every word he said.

"I'm afraid not, Rasul. If you do, I'll come and kill you. The rest of the five Families will kill you," Frankie answered him honestly.

"So, what do I do?"

"You pull the trigger and get away scot free."

"But Frankie, I can't!" Rasul said, beginning to get choked up.

"You can. Now, pull the fuckin' trigger, you fuckin' moolie!" Frankie shouted, but didn't mean one word of it. He was using reverse psychology to make Rasul pull the trigger, because he knew he wouldn't be able to if he didn't. Frankie was tired. He was tired of popping those little pills, and tired of chemotherapy. He just wanted his life to end and for him to not have to suffer or die a slow and painful death. "Pull the trigger, you fuckin' bastard, snake-ass moolie!" And those were the last words ever spoken by the Boss of all Bosses. The bullets hit him in the chest, every last one of them, and Rasul turned to leave as Frankie slid down the wall.

The Game Ain't Fair! he thought, and told Dog to come on.

Ricky Stango heard each word that was said by Frankie and Rasul, and it only fueled his will to live even more. Frankie was a standup guy all the way to the end. He looked over at his brother, Nicky lying lifeless, and used every inch of what he had left inside of him to rise to his knees. He lifted his gun and aimed it at the two men walking away and pulled the trigger. The single bullet tore right through Dog's spinal, cord leaving his legs lifeless.

"I can't feel my legs!" he screamed, and Rasul spun on his heels and emptied his clip into Ricky's body.

"Come on, y'all!" Pretty E shouted. "They're getting closer!" he said about the police sirens, and ran back to help Rasul carry Dog to the car.

They reached their car the same time the police, ambulances and fire trucks made it to what was once Li'l Italy, and drove right past the scene.

Tonight was a night for the records. It would be remembered as one of the bloodiest massacres in history, but most of all, it would be remembered because it was a night an entire Mafia family had been completely wiped out. Questions would forever reign about who did it, or why it happened, as well as the speculations from police officers and media personnel. One thing would hold strong for sure, and that would be the rumors and speculations about Rasul, Dog, Pretty E and their posse. The underworld knew they were responsible for the hit, but authorities could only guess because there was no evidence.

"The Game Ain't Fair!"

■■■■■■

Detective Cohen was even busier now at his desk than he'd ever been before. Lucy's death had to be connected to them in some way or another, because, *For Christ sake!* Cohen thought, *She was found in Pretty E's apartment. But then, why would he kill her when she was carrying his unborn child?* That was the question, so he did background checks on every and anybody close to them, and when Tammy's record popped up from Philadelphia, he knew he had his murderer. Tammy's record extended clear back into her juvenile delinquent days clear up into her adult years, with crimes from everything from assaults to drug charges.

Tammy spent nearly three years in Montgomery County Prison for bad checks and violating probation on an assault charge she caught for stabbing her boyfriend's baby's mother. That charge right there alone was what got him the warrant from Philadelphia police to go and arrest her on charges of first degree murder, but the warrant didn't go into effect until the next morning.

Cohen was just about ready to close out another case in his office and head home when the news about Li'l Italy came across his walkie-talkie. He jumped up, grabbed his keys and headed for Scott Street.

By the time he arrived at the scene, the entire street was blocked off and news vans, reporters, and cameras were everywhere. Body bags were piled on the sidewalk, and firefighters were still bringing bodies out while Cohen was being briefed on the events that had taken place there tonight. The more he listened, the more it sounded so familiar to him. This scene was only a duplicate to the many scenes he investigated while trying to catch Rasul, Dog, and Pretty E, and for some reason he just felt this scene was theirs to. They had done it again, and again it was completely flawless.

Right then and there, Detective Cohen decided to give up on trying to catch them for the first time since he started on them. They were just too good at what they did, but one day they'd slip up. *And I'll be right here to catch 'em,* he thought. For now, he'd just settle with arresting Tammy, Pretty E's girlfriend, on murder charges.

"The Game Ain't Fair!"

EPILOUGE

"Pretty E"

When I got home last night, I felt better than I had in a long time. In fact, I was feeling good... feeling great! Feel me? Me and my boys had just knocked off the Mob. Yeah, the Mob—the Capelli Family—the same muthafuckas that killed my baby, Lucy, and my unborn child. So seeing them dead should help me at least sleep good again.

I dove in the bed with my baby, Tammy, and made some of the best love I'd ever made with her before. I guess I finally realized that she was the one for me. I mean shit, look at all the shit I put her through.

My name is Pretty E. I have never been faithful. I been fuckin' bitches the whole time we been together. Then on top of that, I told her about Lucy, a white girl. You know how sistas are when it comes down to a white girl. I thought for sure it was over between us, but again I was wrong, because my baby stayed. It ain't nuffin' else for me to do but put a ring on my baby's finger. Matter of fact, I'm going to get one tomorrow morning as soon as the stores open up.

I leaned over and kissed my baby goodnight, but I couldn't sleep. I just lay there in the dark and stared up at the sky as I lay on my back and thought about everything that ever happened to me in this game, and realized that the game ain't fair! Just look at all of the shit I lost. Yeah, I'm a millionaire, but was it worth it? I don't know. Let's do the math.

I lost my boy, Hit-Man, I lost my unborn child and his mother, a woman who I loved dearly, and I don't know what's going on with my boy, Dog. Shit, he might not ever be able to walk again. My boy Rasul lost his wife, Tameeka, who was my girl's best friend, and he had to kill off a man who was like a father to him, all behind his love for me. That's a whole lot of losses. The average muthafucka would have crumbled by now, so hell no, the game wasn't worth all that.

I don't know when I fell asleep, but when I was awakened by what seemed to be a thousand police officers with guns in my face, I thought I was dreaming. Man, it was police everywhere!

"Tammy Brown," Detective Cohen shouted, accompanied by Philadelphia police officers. "You're under arrest!"

"For what?" my baby asked him.

"For the murders of Jennifer Vault and her unborn child."

I couldn't believe my ears when he said that shit! "My baby ain't do that shit!" I said, but he replied, "She'll have her day in court," and began to read her her rights.

Right then, as I watched them cuff my baby, I felt the true essence of the statement, *"The Game Ain't Fair!"*

■■■■■■

"Dog"

When I woke up form surgery and saw my wife, Kim and my kids surrounding my bedside, I was reminded of what life was really about. It was about love and family, happiness and success, and I was blessed to have had a chance to receive it all. I smiled at my wife, but by the way she looked back at me I could tell something was wrong. I tried to sit up, but only my top half moved. *Hold up!* I thought. *Let me try this again.* But still my legs didn't move. I looked up at my wife and she lowered her head. I snapped. "What the fuck is going on?"

That's when the doctor came in and gave me the bad news. I'd never walk again. I was wheelchair bound for the rest of my life.

I looked at my wife and kids and the tears wouldn't stop falling from my eyes. I deprived them of a husband and father all because of my selfishness and love for the game. The game and chasing that "bloody money" had left me a cripple. That's when the pain of not being able to be a productive father and husband really hit me.

I looked at my sons and apologized, but they really didn't understand. They were more so worried about me than anything else. They just didn't realize yet, but they would later on, because I wouldn't be able to do the things we used to do together, like race each other, or play basketball. That's what was fucked up.

I did still had my life though, so I was happy in that sense. I was a millionaire, so money isn't an issue. I own a whole slew of property and shit like that, plus I still had the love of my life at my side. My boys, Rasul and Pretty E are okay, and so am I. I'm done with the game. You know why? Because *"The Game Ain't Fair!"* That muthafucka just ain't fair!

■■■■■■

"Rasul"

Wha's up, y'all? I guess it's my turn to tell y'all why *"The Game Ain't Fair!"* to me now, huh? Alright, let me cut this T.V. off first, because this is the fourth time I done watched this same news coverage on this Li'l Italy shit.

Yo, on some real shit, I only got in the game as a youngster on some following my boys shit, and before long, the shit started getting good to me, because I was creating a better life for me and my family, and so was my boys. I still thank Hit-Man to this day for introducing us to the game.

But, as I grew in the game, the more serious it had become. It was like the more money I was making, the more problems came along, you know? Muthafuckas wanted to start trying me and shit. That's why I did that eight years in jail. I did that shit all because of a dice game; a muthafuckin' dice game, and all because my pride was on the line. Shit, I had to bang that nigga, or else other muthafuckas would have started trying me, you know?

Anyway, after I got out of jail my life really started to change because I was a grown man now. I was seeing shit through a grown man's eyes. I had left the prison systems with what I called a "Federal Education". I didn't do State time, I did Fed time, and it's a big difference, although you are still locked up. The difference was that I was locked up with some real muthafuckas, some heavy-weighters who played da game and were the best at playing it. And I'm not just talking about da drug game, I'm talking bad checks, credit cards, insurance fraud, computer hackers, bank robbers, money launderers, kingpins, kidnappers, scam artists, killers, Mob bosses, cop killers... everybody! I even met a muthafucka who ran a fake funeral home! Whatever you could think of as being a scam or a way of getting money illegally, nigga, they were there, and I was like a sponge to each and every one of them. I soaked up everything. I was even around fake preachers who scammed people for millions. So when I say "Federal Education", that's what I mean.

When they first transferred me to McKean Federal Prison from Juvenile Detention, I was put in a cell with a man who y'all came to know as Frankie Maraachi. He became like a father to me over the years, and I grew to love him. That's why it hurt me when I did what I did last night. Anyway, It took me some time, but before long I knew who he was. He was a Mob boss. The coincidental thing was that he was from my hometown, Delaware. Who would'a ever thought that my little city had a Mob? But after a little more research, I found out that it was official, and that the Capelli Family was like the ruthless family out of the five others that existed. But y'all already know that from the first "Bloody Money", so I'm not going to go into detail.

So like I said, y'all, when I got out my life changed. I was hungry, I was educated in all aspects of life, and I was determined to win at all costs. My plan was to get in da game and get out a very rich man, find me a wife, make me some babies, and settle down and enjoy life. But all things ain't as easy as you can plan them, you know? To do all of that and make all of that come true, I knew I would have to do some shit I knew wasn't right. I had to go against my soul. I had to kill, but killing meant coming up, and so I did it. The crazy thing was that even though it meant coming up, it still hurt, feel-me? And I knew that there'd be repercussions I'd have to pay later on in life because of karma, but I was focused on one thing; money. And as a result, here I sit.

Yeah, I'm rich and I live in a huge home. I have so many assets and properties that my wealth skyrocketed to millions. But like I knew it would happen, karma came back to me and claimed my wife, Meek-Meek, and like always, I'm sitting here on her favorite couch staring up at her picture on the wall and wishing I could have her back. Wishing I could have made the other decision, but then I wouldn't have *her*, my precious li'l Meek-Meek, my daughter, the gift Tameeka gave me even though she knew it might have cost her her own life, which it did, but she still delivered it anyway. Now that's love, and I'll forever owe my wife one. That's why I'm really leaving da game. Shit, I gotta be here to raise my kids, Jaquaan and Tameeka.

What I'm trying to say, y'all, is this: If you're in the game and you're not kingpin or at least a nigga getting a couple dollars, give it up. The game has changed. Ain't no need to get a ass-hole full of jail time for a measly couple stacks, feel me? What's a couple thousand? Exactly! It ain't shit, and it damn sure ain't worth no jail time. It's fucked up, because you don't have to just watch out for the police no more, you gotta watch out for the bitches, stick-up kids, and the snitches. It's crazy! It's like snitching is the new thing to do. It's fucked up, but it's happening. Niggaz need to start plucking them muthafuckas off for that bullshit! Feel me!

To sum everything up in a nutshell, I'm going to say this: The game is not a real job, and should not be taken as one. Always look for the other shit to do besides hustle. Use the game as a stepping stone, or a hustle to get you out of a bind or something, but never rely on just it. It's good to know how to hustle, because you'll always know how to get money. But please, take it from a nigga who supplies, and who you buy from. "The Game Ain't Fair!"

And another thing. If you can't do the time, don't do the crime! Its muthafuckas like you who help the police put some real good niggaz behind bars. If I'm talking to you, I'm talking to you!

Peace! I'm out!

Street Knowledge!
"So Real You Think You've Lived It!"

Street Knowledge Publishing LLC
P.O. Box 345
Wilmington, DE 19899
TOLL FREE: 1.888.401.1114
www.skbookstore.com

Date: _____

Purchaser _____

Mailing Address _____

City _____ **State** _____ **Zip Code** _____

Qty.	Title of Book		Price Each	Total
	978-0-9822515-6-0	Bloody Money	$15.00	
	978-0-9822515-9-1	Bloody Money 2	$15.00	
	978-0-9799556-4-8	Bloody Money 3	$15.00	
	978-0-9799556-0-0	Tommy Good Story	$15.00	
	978-0-9822515-0-8	Tommy Good Story II	$15.00	
	978-0-9746199-1-0	Me & My Girls	$15.00	
	978-0-9746199-0-3	Cash Ave	$15.00	
	978-0-9822515-1-5	Merry F$$kin' Xmas	$15.00	
	978-0-9799556-1-7	A Day After Forever	$15.00	
	978-0-9822515-3-9	A Day After Forever 2	$15.00	
	978-0-9799556-2-4	Court & the Streets	$15.00	
	978-0-9822515-5-3	Court In The Street 2	$15.00	
	978-0-9746199-6-5	Don't Mix the Bitter with the Sweet	$15.00	
	978-0-9799556-9-3	Playing For Keeps	$15.00	
	978-0-9799556-3-1	Pain Freak	$15.00	
	978-0-9799556-5-5	Dipped Up	$15.00	
	978-0-9799556-6-2	No Love No Pain	$15.00	
	978-0-9746199-4-1	Dopesick	$15.00	
	978-0-9799556-7-9	Lust, Love & Lies	$15.00	
	978-0-9799556-8-6	Money and Murder	$15.00	
	978-0-9746199-7-2	The Queen Of New York	$15.00	
	978-0-9799556-5-5	Dipped Up	$15.00	
	978-0-9746199-8-9	Sin 4 Life	$15.00	
	978-0-9822515-4-6	A Little More Sin	$15.00	
	978-0-9746199-5-8	The Hunger	$15.00	
	978-09746199-3-4	Money Grip	$15.00	
	978-0-9822515-7-7	Young Rich & Dangerous	$15.00	
		Total Books Ordered	Quantity	
			Subtotal	
	SHIPPING/HANDLING (Via U.S. Priority Mail) $5.25 for 1st book, $2.00 for each additional book		Shipping Total	
	Institutional Check & Money Order (No Personal Check Accepted)	**Total**	**$**